Kinnakeet Stories

Bernie Lewis

More Books by Bernie Lewis

Local Heroes:
Winchester, Virginia 2000 – 2010

The Long Branch You've Never Seen

Kinnakeet Stories

Short Stories Inspired By
The Outer Banks Of North Carolina

Bernie Lewis

For my family and all other lovers of good
beach stories

Table of Contents

Introduction

Kinnakeet is a special place.

Its roots go back to the earliest Native American times on the Outer Banks of North Carolina. As a wide spot and place of great natural beauty on the sliver of land that is Hatteras Island, it was a gathering place and village site long before the Europeans "discovered" it.

The vast majority of Native Americans are gone now, but the other "Kinnakeeters" with deep roots in the village maintain the pride in their homeland that goes back hundreds of years.

The stories in this collection are inspired by the people who have, or may have, lived or visited here. They experience life, and the beauty and challenges of Kinnakeet, in many different ways. Their stories are presented here for your reading pleasure.

Joe Bell

"Excuse me, ma'am. You look like you could use some help." Miguel had been watching her for the last minute as he approached the house on his morning walk.

The lady, struggling with getting a box out of the van, looked to be in her 50's and was more than a few pounds overweight. The box had to be three-feet square and looked heavy.

"No, I'm okay. Thanks," she said, stopping to look in his direction. But then she stepped away from the van for a moment and tried to lean back, apparently to stretch her back muscles. Both hands pushed in at her lower back.

"Well, pardon me for saying so, but you don't look like you're okay," Miguel said. He stepped off the pavement to the sand driveway. "Please, let me give you a hand."

She took a moment to assess him. He looked almost her age, had short-cut dark hair and sunglasses. He was dressed in a gray tee-shirt, light blue shorts, and walking shoes. She decided he looked harmless.

"I guess you're right. I could use a hand. Thank you." She moved another couple steps away from the rear of the van and let Miguel move into position. "I'm Lisa, by the way. And I really appreciate this."

"Miguel," he said. "And it's no problem." He wrapped his arms around the box, noticed there were three other ones, not quite as big behind that one, and pulled, then lifted it out. "Just tell me where you want this," he said as he turned with small steps toward the house.

She guided him inside and had him set the box in the first room to the left of the entryway. He insisted on carrying the other three boxes in, placing them beside the first one at her direction. She hauled in a couple of small boxes from the passenger side seat. "I've got to open these and decide where everything goes," she said as he placed the final box on the floor.

"Just moving in?" he said, taking a moment to look around at the living room where he stood, and the parts of the other three rooms he could see. There was already a lot of furniture and a few plants in the house. It looked fully lived in already.

Lisa looked around her for a moment before answering. "Well . . . yes and no. Oh, I'm sorry. Would you like some water or something?"

"That would be nice," Miguel said, offering a grateful smile. They walked to the kitchen and Lisa retrieved a bottle of water from the refrigerator and gave it to him. He twisted the cap off and took a deep swallow. "That tastes great. I've been walking for about an hour and starting to get a little dry." He took another drink. "So, you were saying about moving in?"

Lisa got another water and lowered herself gently into a chair at the kitchen table. Miguel joined her when she gestured to a chair. "This is . . . was, my mother's house. She died recently and left it to me. She said for several years that I should live here after she died. She actually tried to get me to live with her the last couple years, but I wasn't ready to do that. So . . . I thought I'd try it out for a few months and see how I like it." She leaned forward and stretched her back muscles again. "So, do you live around here?"

"Yeah, I do," Miguel said. "Similar situation to yours, actually. I'm living in my parents house. They moved into an assisted living place near my sister and wanted me to come and live in the house. I can work from anywhere, as long as I have a computer and internet, and I can set my own schedule, so I decided to give it a try. I've been here six months. I'm about two blocks from here. I was just out on my morning walk."

"That's what I should do," Lisa said with a frown. "I've got back problems and my chiropractor said walking would be the best thing for me. I'm going to try to get into that once I get settled."

"Good idea," Miguel said with a nod. "And the sooner the better." He studied her for a moment, then decided to go ahead. "How about tomorrow morning? I'll stop by here about nine o'clock and we'll walk at your pace for as far as you're comfortable. I'd love a walking companion. I'll put in three or four miles before I get here, so I'll get my distance in. Then, I can show you the good walking areas around here."

Lisa debated. What he was proposing was obviously a good idea. And, it would be nice to have someone to walk with and motivate her to get out and go every morning. She didn't know anybody here, besides a couple of her mother's friends, and they were in their 70's and not walkers. Maybe he could help get her a little more comfortable with being in Kinnakeet. But then, on the other hand . . .

"Okay, it's settled," Miguel said, a bemused smile lighting his face as if he was reading her mind. "I'll see you at nine." He stood up, took another swallow of the water, set the bottle back on the table, and walked to the front door.

Despite her ambivalence, Lisa convinced herself to at least give it a try. She was outside, watering the three rows of two-toned red and yellow blooms in the garden on the sunny side of the house, when she spotted him walking briskly down the street at precisely 9:00 a.m..

Since it was already 65 degrees that May morning, she'd forced herself to wear shorts rather than the more psychologically comfortable sweat pants. She knew it was the right decision, since she figured she'd be sweating quite a bit after even a few minutes of walking. She wore an oversized tee-shirt on top, and had a washcloth in the pocket of the shorts.

"Beautiful flowers," Miguel said, as he slowed and turned into the driveway.

"Yes, they are," she said. "My mother loved these and they looked like maybe they needed a drink." She turned off the spigot and joined him in the driveway. With an uncertain smile, she said, "Let's do this, but I may have to take it easy today."

"No problem."

They walked at her speed for about 30 minutes, winding their way, at his direction, through the neighborhood of mostly older houses, coming out on Route 12 briefly a couple times. They talked almost constantly, each becoming more comfortable as they bounced from topic to topic. As they turned back on the street where Lisa's house was, Miguel asked how she was dealing with her mother's death.

"It's been . . . I guess, kind of rough. I miss her, of course, but I had time to prepare. She had lung cancer, one of those unlucky ones who never smoked, but got it none-the-less. Then, later on, it metastasized to her brain. She was pretty bad off toward the end. I moved her from here to my place in D.C., but she was in the hospital within a month, and died two weeks later."

"I'm sure that was rough," Miguel said. "Were you at least able to say your goodbyes?"

"Yes, mostly. But there was one thing left hanging."

"What was that?"

"She always let me know, after my father's death, that she wanted to be cremated. He was, and she kept his ashes. She said a couple times she wanted her ashes to be with his. But, the couple of times I came down here after she moved in with me I looked and couldn't find his ashes. They were in a little ornate, brown box, but I haven't been able to find it anywhere. So, I guess she spread them somewhere, and did who knows what with the box. And then, toward the end when I tried to ask her about it, and where she wanted her ashes to be spread, I couldn't understand what she was saying. The combination of the bad lungs, the tubes, and the cancer in her brain made it very hard to understand her."

"That's really unfortunate," Miguel said, slowing the pace even a little more, aware of her fatigue. "Do you have any clue what she was saying?"

"Well, just a little . . . She was trying to say three words. I'm sure the first one was

Kinnakeet. No surprise there. She loved this place. She and my father used to vacation on the Outer Banks after I left home. They got into a pattern, after a while, of coming here to Kinnakeet twice a year, spring and fall. It was their favorite place on the Outer Banks. Then, after my father died four years ago, my mother bought this house and moved here."

"Good for her," Miguel said. They'd arrived at her driveway, and stood for a moment while Lisa wiped sweat from her forehead. Then she smiled at him and invited him in for a water. Miguel wanted to hear the rest of the mystery, so he readily accepted the invitation. Once they were in the kitchen, and each had their water, he asked, "So, what's your best guess about the other two words?"

Lisa took a seat and motioned for Miguel to do the same. "The second word, I have no idea. Couldn't even guess. But the third word sounded something like 'jubal,' or 'gerbils,' or 'Goebbels'. The first two don't make any sense, and the only Goebbels I know of is the Nazi general during World War Two. Maybe her brain was just too far gone from the tumor to make sense. It did affect the left hemisphere, and the doctors said that's where the language center is."

Miguel was quick to respond. "But the word Kinnakeet you could understand, and that made sense. She would probably want her ashes spread somewhere here."

"Yeah. I'm pretty sure of that. And . . . if I can't figure out the rest, I decided I'd just take her ashes out into the ocean one day and spread them there. Or maybe the sound."

"That seems right," Miguel nodded, then took a drink of water.

Lisa stared out the kitchen window for a few seconds and wiped her forehead. "But, that still leaves the mystery of my father's ashes, and doesn't get her ashes spread with his. Unless, by chance, that's what she did with his ashes."

"Could be. Too bad she never told you what she did with his."

"Yeah. I wish she'd done that," Lisa said.

Miguel finished his water and stood. "Oh well, keep thinking about it. I'll be here nine a.m. sharp in the morning. See you then."

"Okay . . . I guess," Lisa said, pushing herself to her feet. Her voice sounded more strained than excited at the prospect of another walk so soon. Her facial expression matched the voice. "I've got to stretch now. Chiropractor insisted I stretch before and after each walk."

"Good advice," Miguel said as he walked through the living room toward the front door. "I do that every morning."

The next day Miguel was a couple minutes early, with three quick miles already completed. He stood at the foot of Lisa's driveway and did some stretches while he waited. He had two water bottles in loops on his belt. It looked like the flowers Lisa had been watering the day before had perked up a little.

Lisa came out at five after nine and was ready to walk. She said she'd been a little sore after yesterday, but had committed herself to sticking with it.

They walked just a bit farther, as Miguel led her through some additional streets. They looked at, and commented on, houses that they passed, and talked about Kinnakeet. They shared their mutual anxiety about what the area would be like once the tourist season was in full swing. Miguel made some recommendations for restaurants for Lisa to try before they got impossibly busy in another month. He offered, and she accepted, a dinner excursion to his favorite tavern two evenings hence.

When they were back in Lisa's driveway, Miguel pulled the bottles from his belt and gave one to Lisa. She was a bit winded, but holding up well. After they both had a chance for a swig, Miguel asked, "So, have you made any progress on what to do with your mother's ashes?"

"No," she said, the frustration obvious in her voice. "I want to do something with them. I don't want them just sitting in the house. She always talked about wanting my father's ashes some place where they could have some benefit for the earth and a place that was meaningful to her. I know she would want the same thing for her ashes. I just don't know where that would be." She paused for another drink and a quick sweat wipe. "But I do know that's not on a shelf in the living room."

"I'm sure you're right," Miguel said. "But keep thinking about it. At least you know it's somewhere here in Kinnakeet."

Lisa nodded and finished her water. "Well, thank you for the walk. I'm going to head inside now and do my stretching. Then I'm going to unpack the last box and declare myself settled in."

"Good for you," Miguel said, as he finished his water. "I'll see you in the morning again. Nine o'clock." Lisa said her good-by, and Miguel watched as she turned and walked into the house.

As he did so, he got that feeling he occasionally had when there was something gnawing away at his subconscious. He stood, vaguely focused on the house, for a full minute after Lisa disappeared, trying to clear out the muck so whatever was trying to struggle to the surface could find its way there. Just as he gave up and turned to walk away, it struck him. He realized he needed some internet search time before he could be sure, but his gut told him he was right.

He walked briskly home, skipped the usual post-walk stretch and shower, and settled in at the computer. His work responsibilities could wait, too. It took him only three minutes to find what he was looking for and confirm his hunch.

The next morning he was again five minutes early, but this time on purpose. He walked up the driveway and stood at the edge of the flower garden, a radiant smile lighting his face. However, by the time Lisa emerged from the house, he'd decided to put off sharing his theory until after the walk. The exercise was important, too.

Miguel felt somewhat distracted during the walk, but tried to keep the focus on his companion. He listened well enough to keep her talking, and learned a lot more about her job with the government that she'd recently left after 31 years. She talked a little more about her father as well, and how it took her over a year, maybe even close to two, to get over his death. She shared interesting stories about her parents, and how loving they'd been. What he heard only reinforced his certainty of what he was going to tell her.

By the time they got back to Lisa's house, Miguel was aware they'd been walking at a considerably faster pace than the previous two days. That was his fault. She hadn't complained or asked him to slow down, but looked more strained. It was a slightly warmer morning, and the perspiration on her tee-shirt was probably twice what it had been the day before.

During the walk, he'd figured out how he wanted to tell her his theory and the associated legend. As they reached the driveway he said, "I've got something I want to share with you. About your mother. And your father. I've been thinking about it a lot since yesterday, and if you'll indulge me, I think it might be worth your time."

Lisa's expression was quizzical, but she said, "Okay. . . Would you like to come inside?"

"No," Miguel said, "but I forgot to bring water today, so if you could grab us a couple bottles and come back out here I'd appreciate it."

Lisa seemed a bit confused, but nodded and retreated to the house. She was back in three minutes, bottles and wet washcloth in hand. She offered him the washcloth after handing him a water, but he declined. She wiped her forehead and neck.

Miguel stepped to the side of the driveway beside the flowerbed and pointed to the flowers. "I think these flowers may solve the mystery of where your mother wanted her ashes spread. And, if I'm correct, your father's ashes were spread right here."

Lisa looked stunned. "That . . . might be," she mumbled. "But, why?"

Miguel nodded and knelt to touch the closest bloom. "Out here on the Outer Banks, these flowers are called Joe Bell. Sometimes that's shortened into one word – Joebell," he said, then stood back up. "If I'm correct, the words your mother was saying to you about where she wanted her ashes scattered were, Kinnakeet – house – Joebell. Or maybe, Kinnakeet – garden – Joebell."

Lisa stared at him for a moment. She gripped the washcloth so tight moisture ran out on the ground. "That's . . . That's . . . I think you're right! That's probably it! That sounds like what she was trying to say. I think it was probably 'garden'." She stared at the flowers for a moment. "But, how would you know that?"

"It's a matter of putting a few pieces of a puzzle together, and knowing an old legend." Miguel studied her for a moment. She looked physically uncomfortable. "This may take a couple minutes; can I get you a chair you could sit in? I think we should do this out here instead of inside."

Lisa nodded, and wordlessly walked around to the back of the house. She returned a minute later with two large lawn chairs and set them side-by-side facing the flowerbed. Once they were each seated, Miguel continued.

"The legend associated with these flowers goes like this – A man named Joe Bell came to Ocracoke on the Outer Banks in the early 1900s with a broken heart. Depending on which version of the story you choose to believe, either his lady love had left him and married another, or, his wife, a midwife, had died and left him brokenhearted. This flower is a Gaillardia, a type of sunflower, and was his favorite flower. Supposedly, Joe brought a lot of these seeds with him, and both planted them in his yard in Ocracoke, and cast them to the wind wherever he went on the Outer Banks, in tribute to his undying love for his lady. The seeds flourished wherever they landed and spread along the roadsides throughout the

Outer Banks. Over time, people heard the story of Joe Bell and his broken heart, and as the legend spread, different versions evolved. But, the flower became known everywhere around here as the Joe Bell. Before long, people began to dig up the plants or gather seeds and plant them in their gardens as tributes to Joe, as well as in memory of their own lost loved ones."

"Oh my God!" Lisa exclaimed, both hands flying to her chest. "That's so fitting. My mother would definitely do something like that. She must have heard the story after she moved here with my father's ashes and decided that was the best, and most appropriate place for them." She paused for a moment to study the flowerbed in front of her. "Then, after planting the flowers and mixing his ashes in the soil, she could tend to the flowers, and give them the same love and care she gave my father."

"That does sound right," Miguel said. "Maybe she even knew the legend before she moved here. It's possible she heard about it on one of their earlier trips here, and maybe that was a small factor in her decision to move here. Possibly she and your father even talked about planting a garden of Joe Bell flowers and mixing his ashes in the soil."

"Could be," Lisa acknowledged, as she turned to Miguel with a warm smile. "My mother was a romantic like that. She would have loved the legend of Joe Bell. Planting the flowers, and putting his ashes here, would be the perfect way for her to stay connected to my father."

She turned back to study the flowers for a minute. Her voice became soft and peaceful. "I can just imagine her coming out here every day and talking to him. She would also love bringing some of the flowers inside so she could share the house with him, and continue to feel close to him in there."

Miguel sat with the mood for a moment. "I understand they bloom from early spring well into the fall, and come back every year."

"That's perfect. They're perfect," Lisa said as she knelt and caressed the nearest bloom.

After another minute, Miguel said, "So, this is the place?"

"Yes," Lisa answered, as she stood and stared into the garden.

"Are you going to do it today?"

Lisa thought for a moment. "No. I think tomorrow. I want to prepare myself." She turned to look at Miguel. "And, I want you to be here."

Miguel was caught off guard. "Oh! I don't –"

"Yes, please? After the walk tomorrow morning. It would mean a lot to me." She reached over and touched his arm. Her blue eyes pleaded with him.

Miguel reconsidered. After all, he now felt somehow part of this. Him and Joe Bell. "Okay. I'll see you at nine."

The next morning Lisa was in a decidedly sunnier mood. There was almost a glow about her as she walked briskly out the front door at exactly 8:57. It was a slightly cooler day, but still quite pleasant. Miguel was waiting for her.

Their walk that morning was shorter, but faster. Lisa said she was already starting to feel some benefits from the walking and stretching. She talked a lot about her mother's life, and a bit more about her death. Miguel could tell she was emotionally preparing herself for the spreading of the ashes, and was anxious to get to it. He was happy to listen.

Back at the house, Lisa insisted Miguel come inside for just a couple minutes. She explained she wanted to do an abbreviated stretching routine before starting the "ceremony," and didn't want Miguel to have to wait outside. While she went into the bedroom for the stretching, Miguel stretched in the living room.

When she returned after ten minutes, she was carrying a green brass urn, about a foot high, with golden tree leaves engraved on the surface. She'd changed out of the sweaty walking gear into a red and yellow, flower-print knit dress. The flowers were similar to the blooms of the Joe Bell. A yellow sunflower pendant was a perfect match.

"My mother bought me this dress about two years ago," she said. "Now I have a pretty good idea why she would have thought it was so pretty."

"It certainly is nice, and very appropriate," Miguel said with an approving smile. He momentarily wished he'd thought to ask for a few minutes to dash home for a quick change, but then let that thought go. He doubted what he wore would matter.

Lisa nodded. "Shall we?" she said, gesturing toward the door.

They walked to the edge of the garden, and Lisa stood with the morning sun at her back. After a few seconds she turned to Miguel.

"I spoke about my mother at the memorial service we had in Washington after her death. A number of her friends from here came to that. I've already said a lot of things that I wanted to say to her, and about her, so I'll keep this brief." She took just a moment to wipe a tear from her cheek. "I thought for a while last night that I'd write out something to say this morning. But then I decided I'd rather just be here, and say what came from my heart in the moment."

Miguel nodded in silent respect and agreement as she turned back to face the garden. She held the urn tightly with both arms across her chest, and stood silent for a couple minutes.

"Mom, I'm so thankful for all you gave me. You gave me your love, and taught me to love others. You gave me your support, and taught me to support others. You gave me understanding, and taught me to understand others. As an adult, you gave me friendship, and taught me to be a friend to others." She paused and turned to look at Miguel beside her.

"And, it's due to my newest friend, Miguel, that I can put your ashes to rest where you want them to be. Through his wisdom and insight, I know that Daddy's ashes are in the garden in front of me, and a part of the many Joe Bell flowers that you've enjoyed through the years. And I know, absolutely, that's where you want to be. And, it's where you will be. You and Daddy will be together, again, working with each other to produce beauty in the world. Just as you did in the 54 years you were together before he died."

She knelt and gently stroked one of the Joe Bell blooms, then picked up a handful of the sandy soil and let it slowly slip through her fingers back into the garden.

"This garden, this house, this community, and this world will all be better places for what the two of you will do together from this day forward, as long as this garden shall last. And, I pledge to you, that I will take care of this garden, and take care of the two of you, with all my heart and soul, just as the two of you took care of each other, and me, for as long as I am able."

Miguel watched as the expression on Lisa's face turned from solemn to peaceful, then to joy.

She said, "So, Mom . . . it's time. Thank you for the love and everything else in the past, and thank you for the beautiful flowers in the future."

The ever-present coastal winds seemed to settle for a minute as Lisa pulled the lid from the top of the urn and stepped carefully through the garden, scattering the ashes among the flowers as she went. Then, she put the urn down and got the hose to give the garden a light sprinkling, allowing the new ashes to settle into the earth, mixing with the old ones.

When this was done, she returned to stand beside Miguel. A second later he put his arm around her and she leaned into him, with her head on his shoulder.

They let the silence reign for a beautiful few minutes.

For additional information about Joe Bell and the Joe Bell flower legend, simply enter "Joe Bell Flower" into your search engine.

22

Found

Jenn felt her hands shake as she reached out to knock on the door. She knew what to expect and the sudden anxiety surprised her. But it was there none-the-less.

When the door opened, just a few inches, the face that stared at her was both familiar and not. The voice growling, "What do you want?" was not. But then it couldn't have been.

"I want to talk to you, Mr. Sebastian. Please." She'd hardly gotten the last word out before the face disappeared and the door slammed on the foot that she'd hastily inserted in the doorway.

"No one here by that name," the voice snarled back, "Now go away." The man kicked her foot, but could not dislodge it.

Jenn grimaced at the pain signals from her foot, but managed to plead, "Please, Mr. Sebastian. I know who you are. I don't want to bother you. I just want to talk for a few minutes."

"Look," the man said, opening the door half-way, "I'm not your Mr. Sebastian. My name is John Florio. Do I need to show you my I.D. to convince you to leave me alone?" The face disappeared and the door slammed again.

Jenn stood her ground, her throbbing foot firmly against the door frame. "John Florio is a minor character in your third novel, *Time Passages*. You introduced him on page 37 and he made his last appearance on page 63. John Florio is also the name of an Elizabethan Era author and language tutor to the court of James the First. He was a contemporary of Shakespeare. But then, you know that, and that's why you picked his name for your character, and for yourself when you decided to disappear."

From inside came a clear, and obviously irate, "Shit."

Jenn had fired her best shot, and now waited. It was nearly half a minute before the door opened and the famous author she knew as C.H. Sebastian, but who had not been seen in public, photographed, or interviewed in over 15 years, stood before her. He looked just as she suspected he would. He stood slightly above her height of 5'8", though he was slightly stooped, and a few pounds overweight, in contrast to her slender frame. His thinning hair and beard were gray, his face pasty white. He wore well-faded jeans and a flannel shirt with a small hole where the top button used to be. She tried her best not be intimidated by the full-body disdain he shot her way.

"And who are you? Some over-aged English literature student writing your master's thesis on ancient has-been American writers?"

"No," Jenn replied, fixing her eyes on his. "My name is Jenn Simmons, and I already did that. I just want to talk to you."

"Oh, I see. So you can make your name as an investigative reporter by writing a big feature article for the New York Times on the mystery of the once-famous writer who walked away from it all."

"No, Mr. Sebastian. I'm not a journalist. I'm not going to write anything about you or tell anybody I found you. I promise. I just want to talk. To get some questions answered for my own purposes." Jenn waited for a reply but got none. "Don't you think I deserve that for figuring everything out and finding you?"

"No!" was the immediate reply. "What you deserve is a kick in the butt. But then you'd sue me for sexual assault and get famous that way."

The standoff continued for another minute. Then the voice said, "If I let you in I'm probably not going to answer most of your questions. Then you have to leave when I tell you to. And, you have to call me John, or Mr. Florio. Since that's my legal name."

"Agreed," Jenn said without a moment's hesitation. It was several more seconds before the path was cleared for her entry. The living room she entered was small, in keeping with the modest older house just off North Drum Road. The furniture – a sofa, a side-table, two upholstered chairs, two over-stuffed bookcases, and a television, were likely thrift store bargains. But the antique Persian rug was spotless, as was the rest of the room. "I'll call you John, if that's okay," Jenn said.

"Whatever suits you," John said. Jenn picked her spot on the sofa after his command to "Sit."

He took his seat in the chair where his coffee mug rested precariously on the arm. "I'd offer you something to drink," he said, "but you're not going to be here long enough to enjoy it, now are you?"

Jenn returned a bemused smile. She liked him a lot. She was ready to start with the first of her half-dozen or so prepared questions when he interrupted her thoughts.

"Before you start, I get to ask my questions." She nodded her agreement. "I've got to know how you found me so I'll know how many hundreds of other curious and inquiring minds and paparazzi to expect."

Another smile. "Oh, no. No one else is likely to find you. I just figured out that when you decided to drop out that you'd enjoy the tease of picking a name of one of your characters. You wouldn't pick a main character, so I made a list of names of all the minor characters in your five novels. Then I eliminated the female names, left in the ones that could be either male or female, and had 34 names. I did a search of federal, then state data bases using a search engine I modified, concentrating on the southern states, since I figured you wouldn't be comfortable living in the North. I was going to search western states next, but I got hits on quite a few of the names. I narrowed them down by age when I could, then I searched the directories of name change filings and found John Florio in North Carolina. Tracing you to Kinnakeet was really easy after that."

John snarled. "Is all that legal?"

"Mostly."

"In other words, no. So I should throw you out on your tiny little butt right now."

"But you won't," Jenn thought, but dared not say. She noted the second butt reference and recalled this leitmotif from his stories. Instead, she said, "Do you have another question?"

He stared at her. "So, you're an English lit nerd and a computer geek too? That's an unusual combination. Literature nuts usually don't know how to turn on a computer, much less use one."

"I'm the exception," Jenn said. "And that's part of the reason I'm here. After my masters in English lit, I started on a masters in software engineering and systems architecture. Didn't finish it because I solved a problem my professor and a bunch of other programmers were having that was hanging up the widespread use of artificial intelligence. I filed for a trademark for my little brainstorm, then shopped it to two of the biggest chipmakers and let them get into a bidding war. I cleared enough to do what you did after your last novel – dropout for a while, maybe a long while, and take the time to figure out what I wanted to do next."

"And what you wanted to do next was find me?" John said, with a huff and bitter mockery in his tone. "That wasn't very smart."

"Maybe not, but it was what I wanted. You'd been burning inside me for some time."

"That's what my ex-wife said before she left," John replied as he reached for his cup. "Okay, enough of the preliminaries. Let's get this over with. Ask your first question."

Jenn was ready. A smile of success settled across her face. "How much writing have you been doing in the last fifteen years?"

"What makes you think I've been writing? Don't you think I could come up with something else to do?"

"Well, you're a writer. It's in your heart and your soul. It's what you do. You said so at one point, after the fourth novel."

John fixed her with a stare. "What are you now, a shrink as well as a lit and computer freak? If so, you should know that people sometimes change. They grow tired of something and move on to something else."

"Is that what you did? Grow tired of writing?"

"No. Next question."

Jenn grinned. "I'm sure you know, that a couple critics, highly respected ones, said that the protagonist in your last novel, Will Michael, the minister, was as autobiographical as anything you ever wrote. He got frustrated and overwhelmed with his success as a minister and all the increasing demands on him and just escaped. He staged his own disappearance. But after a while of experiencing other things in life, and self-examination, he realized sharing his faith and his message with others was what nourished his own soul. So he came back. He found a different way to share his faith with his congregation. And, I think that makes sense as something you'd actually do. Return to writing."

"Hogwash!" John flailed his hand in front of his face as if swatting away an attacking mosquito.

Jenn continued. "So, my guess is that you've been writing. Maybe you never stopped. Maybe you've been working on that unpublished novel that you were never quite satisfied with."

John sprang from his chair, knocking his empty coffee cup to the floor, and stormed down the hallway toward the back of the house. Jenn expected to be ordered out, but no such demand came. She waited.

Five minutes later John stomped back in the room and glared at Jenn, hands on his hips. "Tell me what you want," he commanded.

Jenn studied his face, trying to decipher if he wanted an honest answer or was setting her up to throw her out on her tiny butt. What she saw was infuriation, but perhaps just a touch of sincerity. She decided to take the chance. Give him at least part of the truth.

"I want to understand. Understand you. I'm at the same point in my life that you were 15 years ago. I've had considerable success. I've made a ton of money. I have the freedom to do what I want. And I want to know, I want to understand, what you've done with that. And how it's worked out for you."

John walked to the window and stared out for a few moments. Then he slammed down in his chair and scowled at Jenn. "You want to know why I walked away? It's because I got tired. Not tired of writing, but tired of the critics. Those assholes who could never write anything half as good as the worst piece of shit I ever wrote, telling everybody whether they should buy my book or not. Telling them what was wrong with every storyline, every character. Telling them that the minister in Finding Grace was really based on me and my inner workings and family secrets. And, that his marriage was a mirror of my marriage." He pulled his eyes away and studied the wall across the room. His tone lost a little steam. "They didn't know me. Ninety percent of them never met me."

From what Jenn had learned researching her thesis there was a lot of truth in those two observations from the critics, but dared not offer that opinion. "I certainly understand," she said, and sat silently to allow the atmosphere in the room to cool.

"And what about you?" John demanded, "Did you study English literature because you wanted to be a writer? Or, God forbid, a critic?"

"No, not at all," Jenn insisted. "I just enjoy reading good stories. Especially when they're told by authors with exceptional writing skills, like you."

John scoffed at her. "Kissing butt will get you nowhere around here, young lady." His face rumpled with disdain. "You're not in graduate school anymore."

"Sorry, but it's true. For me, reading a good story, well written, is like –."

"Well, good for you. Now, do you have another question or are we done?"

"You still haven't told me what you've been doing these 15 years, but maybe if you're not ready to talk about that you can tell me why Kinnakeet? You could live anywhere."

John looked at his watch. "I can answer that if you want to take a short walk with me. But, you've got to promise me two things." He counted them off with his fingers. "One, not to say a word after we leave this house. And two, to leave me alone after our walk."

"Agreed," Jenn said, surprised at the offer. There was always tomorrow.

The walk took them down the street to North Drum Road, then a few yards to an elevated wooden walkway. John led the way up the steps, then out the 50 yards or so over the marshy vegetation and water to the edge of the sound. They climbed down the steps, then John grabbed a well rusted aluminum lawn chair tucked under the stairway. He pulled it open and deposited it in the sand a couple feet from the edge of the water. He nodded to the chair and instructed Jenn to "Sit." When she was seated, he pointed to the horizon and said, "Now be quiet and learn."

Jenn studied the scene in front of her. The top edge of the sun, just peeking over the horizon, was inflamed. It ignited the wispy clouds in a pallet of warm reds, oranges, and yellows. Her eyes found a pelican perched on an abandoned pier support sticking out of the water. Gentle waves of cobalt colored water settled just ahead of her feet. The only sound was the gentle "too, too" of a group of shore birds flittering in the marsh grasses behind her.

With John sitting awkwardly in the sand beside her, she watched as the sun disappeared, providing a smoothly transforming tableau of softening hues in the sky. The astonishing performance lasted 20 minutes, ending with only a hint of blushing light left in the sky.

When John said, "Time to go," she was slow to get to her feet. He replaced the chair behind the steps and led the way out. His only words on the walk back to the house were, "Every sunset is different. As is every sunrise."

When they arrived, he stopped beside her car in the sandy driveway and said, "Now go."

Jenn beamed her gratitude for the experience and said, "I'll be back tomorrow."

"Not before ten o'clock, you won't," John shot back as he headed for the front door.

To Jenn's surprise, at 10:15 the next morning the door opened just a few seconds after her gentle knock. Wordlessly, John stepped aside and ushered her inside. After his slightly less demanding, almost suggestive, directive that she "Sit," he asked, "And what do you want today?"

"I want to read what you've been writing." Jenn's confident smile was well rehearsed.

"You're still on that kick?" John's face screwed into a scowl. "What makes you so sure I've been writing? And don't give me that, 'It's what you do' crap."

"Okay . . ." Jenn studied the room for a beat, "You can't just watch sunrises and sunsets all day, although I get it. That was pretty spectacular yesterday, and living here in Kinnakeet is as good, and likely better, than living anywhere else if you want to hide out. But . . . you have to do something with what goes on inside you. I'm sure the sunrises and sunsets alone are stirring powerful emotions inside you. Making you feel, making you think. And human nature is to do something with that. Something expressive, creative. I see no evidence that you're doing anything else with all that, like painting or making beautiful objects. So, it's got to be coming out of you somehow. And yes, damn it, writing is what you do." Jenn pinned her crossed arms across her chest and glared.

John glared right back at her. Finally he said, "So, madam shrink, if I tell you I've been writing, what's your next question going to be?"

"That's easy. I'm going to want to know what you've been writing."

"Figured," John hissed. After a moment he said, "And if I don't tell you are you going to blackmail me? Threaten to tell the world where I am and ruin what little life I have left?"

"No!" Jenn said. "I promised you yesterday, and I'll promise you again today, I'm not going to tell anybody I found you. I'm just . . ." her face went slack, "going to be disappointed in you. That would mean you're not the sensitive, kind person I believe you are. I'm pretty sure this gruff old guy routine is just an act."

Again, John stared at her, seeming to take her measure. "Not as much of an act as you might think," he finally said. "You have no idea what these last few years have been like for me." After a moment, he dropped his chin, fixed her in a stare, and added, "Nor am I going to tell you."

Jenn knew a little about that. Both of his parents had died a decade ago, two years apart. The paparazzi, and a couple members of the press, had staked out the funerals. Expecting at the first one, and hoping at the second, that he would make an appearance.

John turned toward the kitchen, took a step, then said, "There's coffee if you'd like some." After Jenn declined he proceeded to the kitchen, returning a couple minutes later with coffee for himself and a bottle of water for Jenn.

"Did you see the sunrise this morning?" he asked after handing her the bottle and taking his seat.

"I did," she said. Her cheeks pushed upward. "It was beautiful."

"It always is," he nodded. "I've yet to see one that didn't make me think that somehow, despite all the evidence to the contrary, there must be a God who is trying to tell us something. Something about splendor and hope."

Jenn bowed her head a couple degrees in agreement.

"So," John said as he pushed himself forward in the chair, "what do you know about this supposed unfinished novel of mine?"

Jenn felt the cosmos shift. "Not much, but then nobody does. Supposedly you made a comment after *Finding Grace* that maybe now you could finish a piece that could be your best work of all. The media people assumed it was a novel, and, since there was six years between the publishing of *Breakfast Harmonies* and *Finding Grace*, that you probably had been working on it then, and set it aside. But then, there were the disbelievers who thought you were pulling everybody's leg."

"Of course," John grunted, "there are always disbelievers. It's the nature of the game. If there's nothing to say, make something up and try to create controversy."

"Have you finished it?" Jenn asked, leaning forward, tossing the water bottle between her hands.

"And if I told you I had?"

Jenn hadn't anticipated this. She was prepared for continued resistance, dodging and weaving. She had to think for a moment. "I'd want to read it."

"Ha!" John's head shuddered. "And what would be the point of that?"

It took Jenn just a moment. "I suspect that you haven't let anyone read it. Have you?"

When John remained silent and motionless she continued. "We know that every writer needs readers. Someone who can be objective and offer feedback. Someone who can run it through another set of eyes, another brain, another set of life experiences. Not like a critic, but like a . . . well, like John Q. Public who will buy the book and read it with an expectation of being entertained, or enlightened, or challenged. I can do that for you. I promise. Fair and honest."

John grew rigid. His face tightened. "Go away," he snapped.

"But I . . ."

"Leave! Now," he said, pointing at the door.

Jenn pushed herself, slowly, to her feet. She placed the water bottle on the end table. As she opened the door, she heard a mumbled, "Meet me at the sunset." Her steps vaulted as she slipped wordlessly out the door.

John arrived before she did and had the chair waiting for her. "Not a word!" he admonished as Jenn lowered herself into the seat. She knew her galloping heartbeat was only partially from the walk to the sound.

The sunset was as impressive as the night before, but Jenn's attention wandered. As the last light neared extinction, John rose to his feet. Jenn did the same. After replacing the chair, John led the way back to his house.

In the driveway he turned to Jenn and said, "I suppose you have a computer in the house, or room, or wherever you're staying?"

"I do," Jenn said, a shiver echoing through her.

John reached in the pocket of his jeans and extracted something. He grabbed her hand and placed the object in her palm. Jenn bolted her hand, wrapping her fingers around a thumb drive.

"Thank you!" she said as John pulled away and disappeared through the doorway.

She read through the night, assisted by three cups of coffee.

The story was of a Black man's tortured relationship with a daughter he'd fathered with a white woman outside his marriage. The marriage was childless; his wife a kind, but infertile soul. The mother of the child was accommodating of his desires to see the little girl, in return for regular, secret child support payments. That is, until she moved 500 miles away when the child was six-years-old. His contact after that was irregular. His anguish and guilt were not.

Since the age of 20, when he began his trade as a cabinet maker, he'd wanted nothing more than to be a father. His heart expanded with each visit with the adoring child, and shriveled each time he left her. He existed for little more than to see his little girl. Each visit carried him through the next few days, then he labored through bouts of depression and angst until the next surreptitious visit could be arranged. His wife eventually left him, never knowing the true reason behind his increasing detachment.

His daughter loved him with all her heart and, he believed, shared his torment during his absences. When her mother moved again, when his daughter was nine, she left no forwarding address and cut off all contact between father and daughter. For the next three years, the man searched for her in every way he knew. Unsuccessfully. He was left only with the hope, that when she was an adult, and freed from her mother, she would find him. He lived only for that day.

The story ended the night before her eighteenth birthday. He was brimming with hope. His house was filled with gifts he'd bought her. There was also a series of wood carvings he'd made for her over the years, depicting loving fathers and daughters, preserved for her eyes only.

Jenn found the writing to be concise and captivating. Character development was engrossing. Throughout the story, themes of racism and stereotypes were explored. But the joys and pain of a father's deep-seated love and devotion propelled the tale thrillingly forward. It was a rollercoaster ride of gut wrenching emotions. Jenn was raw and drained when she finished the last page.

She hadn't slept when she knocked on John's door at 10:30 in the morning. When he opened the door she stammered, "I knew her!" Then, through a burst of tears, "And don't try to tell me that's not based on you." She pushed by John into the house.

Before John could ask, she began. "We were eight-years-old. We were in the same class in school. She used to tell me that her real father was famous. She didn't live with him, but she saw him several times a year when he would come and take her to special places. I didn't really believe her. She had a father, or at least a father figure, who lived with her. I thought she was making it all up. I didn't really care. Then, one day, she wrote her real father's name down and gave it to me. It meant nothing to me, but I put it away in a drawer, along with a picture of her she gave me."

When she paused for a breath, John was pacing the floor in front of her. He stopped and immediately urged her, "Go on!"

"I forgot all about it and she moved away before long. When I was cleaning out things in my old bedroom in my parents' house after graduating from college I found the slip of paper with your name on it and her picture. I'd heard of you, and read a couple of your books during college. And that's when I got interested in who you were. When it came time to come up with a topic for my master's degree thesis I choose you. You had disappeared by then and I thought it would make a great research project to gather together all that was known about you and your life. So that's what I did. But there was nothing out there, anywhere, about Lisa. I figured maybe she did just make it up, or her mother told her that as a way to try and make her feel important."

"Yes . . ." John nodded, his face reddening. "Lisa was her name. Lisa Sawyer. I don't suppose you stayed in touch?" He grabbed the back of the sofa for support.

"No."

"Well, of course not." John stepped around, then slumped into, the sofa.

Jenn rushed to sit beside him and put her hand on his shoulder. "But I bet I can find her."

They talked for a few minutes about the pros and cons of trying to locate Lisa. John acknowledged both sides of the issue. As much as he wanted to contact her and renew their relationship, he also could see how she might not want this. Eventually they agreed that if Jenn could find Lisa with her computer skills she would make the initial contact and determine whether Lisa wanted to meet her father. If the answer was "No" she would not disclose to John where Lisa was.

Before leaving to start the search, Jenn informed John that the story was one of the most poignant and heart-rending she'd ever read. She insisted that he give serious consideration to contacting his agent and starting the process to have it published. John dismissed the idea, but agreed that they would discuss the story and the writing later.

It took Jenn three hours to find Lisa, now Aubrey. It was a change of name document in West Virginia that connected her to Aubrey Conner. The document had been filed with the state when Lisa was nine, probably shortly after she'd moved and contact with John was stopped. John had not given Jenn the name of Lisa's mother, but Jenn suspected she'd changed her name as well, as there was another change of last name from Sawyer to Conner filed at the same time. Perhaps the result of a marriage.

In another hour Jenn located an Aubrey Conner who was probably the right age living in Hagerstown, Maryland. She had the address and a phone number a minute later. She gave herself a few minutes to think through how she would approach Aubrey, on the phone, with the news. However, she didn't want to put the contact off and give herself time to reconsider.

She made the call. When a woman answered she began with, "I'm sure you don't remember me . . ."

The meeting took place at Aubrey's home two days later. Many tears were shed by all parties, including Jenn, who stayed for just a few minutes before going for a walk to allow some privacy. They'd discussed leaving a copy of the novel draft for Aubrey to read, and John decided to do this after telling her about it and her request to read it.

On the seven-hour drive back to Kinnakeet, the novel was discussed in detail. With Jenn's feedback, John warmed to the idea of publication. When Aubrey gave her enthusiastic approval a week later, the decision was made. Everyone agreed it was highly unlikely anyone could identify the autobiographical elements of the story, though of course there would be speculation. Aubrey wanted only an autographed copy; John insisted she would receive half of the royalties.

John and Aubrey began regular visits. Jenn worked with John remotely to prepare the novel for submission to his old editor, who was thrilled to work with him again.

When the book, by C. H. Sebastian, was published nine months later, the story ended with a knock on the father's door at noon on the day of his daughter's eighteenth birthday.

The book was well received by the critics. Mostly.

45

Mudball

No one is sure anymore when the tradition of mudball began or whose brilliant idea it was. It has been around for at least as long as Buddy and Sissy can remember, and they're both in their 60s.

According to legend, the Midgetts and the Newtons held an end-of-the-tourist-season picnic the Sunday after Labor Day weekend, starting at least 60 years ago. Back in those days, the season was pretty much over by then, and most everyone could get free for the event. About 15 years ago, as the season on Hatteras Island expanded well into September, the picnic and mudball game were moved to the second Sunday in October.

The gathering has always been at the Kinnakeet park where there are now seven picnic tables, in addition to the ball field. There is usually anywhere from 40 to 50 family members, a few friends, a fiancé or two, or others who just drop by, in attendance. The folks come from every village on the island, and even a handful of family who now live on the mainland come for the occasion. Of course, there are children of all ages present, and lots of games for them. But the game of mudball is restricted to those 16-years-old and up.

It is often those who turn 16 the year before who are most excited about playing in the game. It's like a rite of passage they highly anticipate and nearly all of them play.

But as you might expect in such a large group, there are also a few of the older players who, for reasons of their own, look forward to the game as the highlight of the year. At least Frank and Willie, the brothers Newton, feel that way. They have each been the "victims" of the mudball. Frank last year and Willie five years earlier. They have also each been lucky enough to be the "caller."

Some years it's hard to field two teams of at least eight players each. But most years there are enough brave souls to fill the infield and outfield positions. Sometimes there are even a few extras.

The game is basically baseball or softball, played with a tennis ball. The batter uses a tennis racket instead of a bat. Pitching is always underhanded and the ball is lobbed, so it's basically a lot like slow-pitch softball.

Many of the guys, and quite a few of the girls, can really smack the ball, so long fly balls to and through the outfield are common. Larry Midgett and Joe Clark are known for their awe-inspiring drives that probably would end up in the left field seats in Turner Field. Denise Newton, who was a standout on the high school girls' tennis team until her graduation two years ago, can hit the ball farther than about 98 percent of the guys.

Since the game is played on Kinnakeet Field where there is no outfield fence, when those big-hitters come up to bat, the cry, "Go back. Way back!" echoes through every corner of the park. Each of the outfielders, and at least a couple of the infielders, run back to the edges of the grass and hope for a chance to catch the long fly ball for an out.

The special features of mudball that make it the crowning feature of the picnic, and the entire day, are the preparation, storage, and eventual pitch and hit, of a tennis ball covered with mud until it is the size of an extra-large softball. The techniques involved in making the mudball (and a spare, just in case), have been handed down over the years and are part of the pre-meal tradition.

Two members from each family are charged with bringing two Solo cups filled with dirt, and just the right amount of muck from the marsh at the edge of the sound. (The exact mixture is known only to those privileged to supply the substance.)

At the appointed time, before everyone sits down to fried chicken, a variety of seafood dishes, baked beans, coleslaw, and a plethora of deserts, the mud is mixed and two tennis balls, typically older, well-used ones, are coated with the substance. Once the mud is pounded, packed, and smoothed into place, the balls are sealed in a ziplocked freezer bag and carefully placed, along with a latex glove, in someone's cooler, along with their ice and jugs of lemonade and sweet ice tea. It's essential the balls be kept at the right temperature until it's time for, hopefully, only one of them to be used.

After everyone is stuffed from the shared hour-long lunch feast, the teams are chosen. The two team captains take turns with their picks and must alternate choices between the two families, resulting in teams roughly evenly populated with members of each family.

It was decided many years ago, well before my time, that there would be no family versus family rivalries. Memories of the Hatfields and McCoys were no doubt still fresh when this decision was made. Ladies are especially encouraged to play and several come prepared each year with gloves and rackets.

After the teams are chosen, but before the game begins, an old Atlanta Braves ball cap is brought forth. As long as I've been old enough to know what was going on, my grandmother, Marie Midgett, has been the keeper of the hat and the marbles that go with it. She was awarded this honor after winning the "Bake-off" contest three years in a row that was held way back when at the picnic. Her fried chicken, seafood gumbo, and key lime pie were the winners those three years.

Marie puts one marble in the hat for each player. All of the marbles are white except for one brown one. One at a time the players are called up to where Marie stands on home plate, and pick a marble from the hat held over her head. They take a quick look at it in their hand, then put it in a pocket in their shorts or pants. Once everyone has a marble the game can begin.

The game of mudball proceeds like a regular baseball or softball game – there are three outs to an inning; however there are no called strikes, and swings and misses are rare. The "ping" of the ball exiting the racket when contact is made brings shouts of excitement from the many on-lookers every time.

The special rule of the game comes into play once the game passes the third inning. During the fourth inning or later, the holder of the brown "mudball" marble, while in the field, can shout, "mudball!" at any time and display their prized possession. This signals that the next player scheduled to come to bat gets the "privilege" of hitting the previously prepared mudball.

Of course, this being the South, the ladies are excused from this assignment. There has been discussion of changing this rule over the last few years, but a critical mass has not yet been reached. Maybe soon. Interestingly, it's the ladies who have been the strongest proponents of the change.

Of course, the timing of the "Mudball!" call has always been a topic of great discussion, both in the couple of minutes it takes to get everything ready, and often for weeks afterward.

In the years that I can remember, a wife has called it on her husband, and a man called it on his boss. A mother has called it on her son. My cousin Andy called it on his best friend. Apparently, they had an agreement that if one got the brown marble they would call it on the other. Danny Newton called it on his brother, Tommy. From Tommy's reaction, I don't think they had an agreement about this ahead of time.

Whoever the lucky (?) person is who gets called, the crowd always responds with cheers and shouts of anticipation. Except maybe the year, I think four years ago, when Annie Clark called it on her ex-husband, Joey Newton. He had married her cousin about a month after their divorce. The crowd initially groaned when that call was made but then got more into the spirit of the moment. If I recall correctly, the majority of ladies in attendance were the ones who cheered the loudest. But, to his credit, Joey accepted the mud shower like a true gentleman, even though Annie probably didn't consider him one.

After the call is made, the game is stopped while the cooler is ceremoniously brought to the pitcher's mound. The pitcher is supplied with an extra-large yellow rain slicker and catcher's mask brought out by Marie. The batter is not allowed any additional or special attire. Then, the pitcher (who can be anyone already on the field), takes the mudball from the cooler and bag. He or she is allowed to wear a latex glove on their pitching hand if they'd like.

At this point the catcher and home plate umpire disappear from behind the plate, and the infielders and outfielders either decide to "play deep" or simply exit the field.

So, once all the preliminaries are out of the way, and the hooting and hollering reach a fever pitch, the ball is lobbed from half-way between the mound and the plate, and the batter takes his swing.

As you would expect, the result is quite a spectacle. When the ball is prepared properly, as it is about 95 percent of the time, an area within about a 30-foot radius of the point of contact is bathed in an explosion of mud, and the whole area, especially the batter, is a mucky-muddy mess.

The batter knows that his reputation, for at least the following 12 months, and maybe years to come, especially as prior years are recalled on the day of the picnic, will be determined by how hard he swings, and how solid the impact between ball and racket is. The consequences of a weak swing or poor contact are not going to be pleasant. And God forbid he misses the ball, and the backup mudball ball is needed.

On the other hand, a massive swing and full, center-of-the-racket contact with the mudball, will likely be rewarded in a variety of ways by both the Midgetts and the Newtons for the coming year. There have been reports of regular deliveries of pies, cookies, world-class bar-b-que, and even moonshine. Raises in pay at work and promotions have also been known to occur.

The batter, if he is lucky, closes his eyes just before the moment of contact. If he is even luckier, he wore his glasses or sunglasses up to the plate before the callout was made.

What actually happens to the tennis ball after impact is of little consequence. It is the huge spray of mud, and the reaction of the batter, that the crowd celebrates.

It was determined many years ago that the hilarity that ensues immediately after the "thud" of contact between racket and ball effectively brings the game to an abrupt end. The final score, and who won and who lost, is of no matter. Nobody keeps a tally from year to year. However, the batter is awarded the coveted "Mudball Trophy," and keeps it in his possession for the next year. That is, of course, after he is given a towel and a chance to wipe off, at least a little.

All of this went through my head as I stood at the plate and watched Carl Newton go through the ritual of retrieving the mudball from the cooler and, with a ruthless grin on his face, start his patented windup. Meanwhile, his daughter, my girlfriend Cassie, watched from 10 feet behind second base, with a devious smile on her face, as she excitedly showed me, and everyone else, the brown marble rolling between her fingers.

58

Coming Home

She didn't know much. She only knew he was coming home and she was asked to help him.

After the phone call, she made the slow walk over to the house and was waiting for him when the black Cadillac pulled up. The driver got out, came around to the passenger side, and opened the backseat door. She hardly recognized the young man when he pulled himself out of the door. He'd always been thin, but now it looked like there was little more than skin and bones beneath the bright green and pink long-sleeved shirt and silver pants. A black cap, with "Forty-Niners" embroidered in red, protected the top of his head.

She moved as quickly as she could down the short walkway, and when she reached out to help him walk into the house he put his hands up to stop her.

"No, Miss Hattie. Let me do this by myself."

After the driver pulled a walker from the trunk of the car, he slowly made his way to the front steps. It took him almost a half-minute to negotiate the four wooden steps to the porch. Once he made it, he painfully lowered himself into one of the two weather-stained plastic stacking chairs on the porch. "Let me rest here for a minute," he said, with a grimace in Hattie's direction.

The driver, without a word to him, or her, pulled two suitcases from the trunk, deposited them brusquely on the curb, then got back in the car and drove away.

After a minute or so to catch his breath, the young man turned to Hattie with a weak smile. "Thank you for being here and helping me," he said.

"Happy to be of help, Mr. Sammy."

"Oh, no. We're not doing that," he said, briefly waving an index finger at her. "Got to get that straight right now. My name is Sam. The day I left here I stopped letting people call me Sammy. That's a child's name. My mother will never stop calling me that, but everyone else calls me Sam. And there's no need for the Mister."

With an agreeing smile and a nod, Hattie answered. "Okay. I think that's right, Sam. Good for you. And you just call me Hattie."

With a dip of his head, Sam said, "I'll try. But we've got a lot of history to undo. I know you've always called me Sammy, and I called you Miss Hattie since I was about four years old and you started taking care of me. And now, here we are and you're taking care of me again. I'm 23 now, and I still think of you as the parent figure I respected the most."

"Well now," Hattie couldn't suppress the smile. It was nice to be appreciated. And, she wasn't surprised. "Your folks did the best they could."

Sam's biting laugh was harsh. "Sure they did."

They both sat still for a moment and watched an old beat-up pickup truck pass, followed by a string of youngsters swinging side-to-side on bikes. It was one of those perfect fall afternoons in Kinnakeet when everyone who could be outside wanted to be.

Sam broke the silence. "So, what did my mother tell you about me?"

"She just said you were sick. And you needed a place to stay and someone to look in on you and help you. She said I would cook, clean, and maybe just help you with a few other things."

Again, Sam spit out a laugh that displayed the way he felt about his mother.

"That sounds like her. She didn't tell you the half of it. I probably need a nurse more than I need a cook or housekeeper. But she's not about to pay someone to do that. She'd rather pay you next to nothing and just get as much out of you as she can. Just like she always did. That was always her attitude toward the help. Especially the Black help."

"Oh, now. It's okay, Sam. I wouldn't be here if I didn't want to help."

"Well, thank you. But I need to know. How much is she paying you?"

Hattie hesitated. She thought that was between her and Mrs. Hanson. But she needed to be on good terms with Sam. She decided there was no reason for him not to know. "Fifty-cents an hour above minimum wage."

"So that's . . .?"

She wasn't sure if he was trying to do the math or waiting for her to tell him. She didn't need to work it out. "Three eighty-five an hour."

Sam's head jerked back and forth. He started to say something, but then pulled a large white rag of some kind from his pocket and coughed into it for a full minute. The cough was deep and phlegmy. Finally, when he was able, he said, "That's nothing . . ." he coughed again and wiped his mouth, "to take care of a dying man."

After a moment of shock, mixed with confusion, Hattie said, "Oh, Sam. You're not dying." She meant to sound reassuring, but felt guilty for the thought she had when he first got out of the car that he looked half dead.

"Yes I am," Sam replied, his tone almost defiant. "Probably not today. No promises about tomorrow, though."

Hattie studied his face, looking for some clue – a slightly lifted eyebrow, an upturned lip, anything that could mean he was kidding. But there was nothing. Nothing but hollow cheeks and a pair of bleak, slightly bloodshot eyes staring back at her. "Why?" was all she could think to say.

"Look," Sam said, after a few seconds, "can we not do this right now?"

Hattie wanted to shout at him. He couldn't tell her he was dying, maybe even soon, and not explain why. If she was going to take care of him, in place of his mother, who should have him under her protective wing, but who had all too often abdicated her role over the years, due to "nerves," leaving Hattie to take over, she had a right to know. But, she let the urge pass with just an acquiescing grunt.

They sat in awkward silence for a minute. Then Sam suggested they go in the house so he could lay down, saying he'd had a long day. He struggled to his feet, then Hattie held the screen door as he deliberately made his way inside, lifting and leaning heavily on the walker in front of him.

Once inside, in the small living room just through the door, Sam stopped, and after looking around for a moment, asked, "Did this house just happen to be vacant, or did my parents kick someone out?"

It was hard for Hattie to shift gears so quickly. But she had to try. She was the kind of person who always tried to do the thing that

Jesus would want her to do. "There was a family living here. They'd rented the place for some time."

"A Black family, I assume?"

"Yes," Hattie said, slipping her hands into the pockets of her dress. "That's 'bout all there is on these two streets. The Jackson family lived here. She's my cousin."

"I'm really sorry," Sam said as he shook his head, keeping close eye contact. "They shouldn't have done that."

For another moment he studied the freshly painted off-white walls and furniture of his new living quarters. The upholstered love seat and not-quite-matching chair that almost filled the room looked used-furniture-store new. The carpet was new, but it was bargain basement quality. The room smelled like cheap glue. A 17-inch TV sat on a small cabinet, centered between a box fan and a black telephone.

"And after they evicted them they fixed the place up. Right?"

Hattie simply nodded, then after a few seconds said, "Yes. It needed quite a bit of work. Your folks wanted it nice for you."

"But not for the Jacksons," Sam muttered as he turned toward the hallway.

There was barely room for the walker, but he made it the few steps to the door of the first of the two bedrooms then stopped. "I remember being in this house once before. I was here right after my parents bought it. I might have been about six or seven then. They were having some work done to it and I rode my bike down here to watch. I was in here for a few minutes before I got chased out.”

Hattie motioned to the door beside him and said, “This is the room they fixed up for you.”

Sam stepped in and looked at another set of freshly painted walls, a double bed, dresser, and ocean blue area rug that covered part of the old wooden floor. The sharp smell of paint suggested the room had been finished in the last day or two. “This isn’t much different, and maybe even a little better, than what I was living in before,” he said. He made it to the bed and collapsed. With a bit of a struggle, he got his feet around to lay on the old quilted bedspread and smirked at Hattie.

“Home, sweet home,” he said tersely. Then after a few seconds he closed his eyes and mumbled, “Why don’t you give me a few minutes?”

“Can I fix you something to eat?” she asked. She was making progress lifting the cloud his comment about dying had deposited inside her.

He simply shook his head one time without opening his eyes.

Hattie nodded and closed the door as she left. She retrieved the suitcases from the front curb and, for the moment, left them in the empty second bedroom. She decided to bake a pan of chocolate brownies, knowing that used to be one of Sam’s favorites. She’d stocked the kitchen the day before with the necessities, and enough for a couple starter meals, dinners and breakfasts, as well as a few treats. She figured they'd talk about what he was eating these days after he got there. Mrs. Hanson had given her $45.00 for the kitchen basics and first week's food. She'd spent $65.00.

The brownies were cooling on the counter when Sam made it back to the living room. Their aroma had replaced the unpleasant bouquet of the carpet. He settled on the love seat and sat for a moment, letting his lungs catch up.

"You know," he said after a minute, "technically, I own this house."

"No, I didn't know that," Hattie said as she sat in the chair opposite him.

"Yeah, a couple years ago my dad got into some kind of tax or financial trouble and called me to say he was going to transfer this house into my name. He never really explained why, but a few days later the papers came and I signed them and mailed them back. Of course, I never got any of the rent money, or anything like that after. But, I didn't want anything. It's never been mentioned after that. Even when he decided I should come back to Kinnakeet." He stopped to catch his breath. "I'm not sure exactly how that happened, but I know it was decided between the two of them, mostly my mom, that I should be here, in this house."

Hattie said, "I was wondering why you wouldn't be livin' in your parents' place. There's certainly plenty of room for you there."

Sam chuckled and shook his head. "You think? Four empty bedrooms! But, I know my mother doesn't want me there. And that's fine with me. I wouldn't want to live there with her either. Can you imagine? She'd be a wreck every minute of every day. More so than she usually is. And I'd be miserable living there under her constant disapproval. I'm much better off here, alone." He took a noisy breath. "Except for you."

For the first time, a smile crossed Hattie's face. "Well, this house may make you some real money someday," she said. "One of the real estate companies and a developer want to buy up all the houses on these two streets and move all of us folk out and tear these houses down. They want to build big fancy vacation homes, likes over on the ocean side. They've already been talking to folk, including me and Herbert, and I understand have made some offers. Of course, we've got nowhere to go, and I don't think anyone's sold. Yet. Probably just a matter of time. But there's no place else for us to live here in Kinnakeet, or anywhere else on the island. Our roots, and our ancestors, are here just like a lot of white folks' are."

Sam shook his head. "Don't ever sell out to the bastards! This place needs all you people here a lot more than it needs more big mansions." A coughing spell hit, but a short one this time. After he put the rag back in his pocket, he said in a callous tone, "There's a lot of unhappy people in those big houses along the beach."

It sounded to Hattie like he needed to talk. She could certainly understand, given what she knew about his parents from years of being in the home a few hours every week. There had never been much joy in that house. "You said your father decided you should come back here?"

"Yeah. He came out to San Francisco about five weeks ago. That was the second time I was in the hospital. He talked with the doctors, and when he got the lowdown about my condition and prognosis, he decided I should be here where someone could keep an eye on me. Of course, that wouldn't be him since he spends about 99% of his time in D.C., and it would be 'inconvenient' for him to have me there." Sam studied Hattie for a moment. "I don't know if you know anything, but I'm convinced he has a girlfriend there, and maybe even another family."

Hattie shook her head. "I don't know nothin' about that." She wasn't always completely truthful when she thought the truth would hurt someone. But, she always felt a little guilty when she fibbed.

"Well, I don't blame him. If I was married to my mother I'd have a girlfriend or another wife somewhere else too. I always figured if I hadn't been born he'd have divorced her years ago. But, it might have been nice to have him around a little more when I was growing up."

He stopped to grab for a couple breaths. "I bet he hasn't been here much at all since I left home."

Again, Hattie shook her head, but remained silent this time. She knew he'd come home only three or four times a year in the last five years, and depended on her for twice-a month phone calls to update him on his wife. She got an additional check every three months for her time. He'd also informed her he'd send an extra $50.00 a week for her care of Sam while letting his wife take responsibility for her basic pay.

"So, if I remember right," Hattie said, anxious to shift the conversation in a slightly different direction while still letting him talk, and maybe learn a few things at the same time, "you left home shortly after graduating from high school."

"Yeah, that's right. There really wasn't anything for a person like me here. I was anxious to get away from home and the battles with my mother. I figured the farther away the better, so when I got into UCSF I was ready to go. I knew San Francisco would be a good place for me, and I'm sure my mother was just as happy to have me gone."

Hattie thought about defending his mother one more time, but decided against it. She'd made her bed. "And so how'd that go?" she asked. She knew the basics, or at least his mother's version of them. She suspected she was about to hear a very different story.

"School itself, not so good. But classes in the theater department were great. I had to take some required freshman classes, but I had two electives I could choose each semester, so I took a dance and an acting class each semester. That's where I really found myself. I only lasted one year in school, but the theater professors and other students had connections in the community, so I did some acting and dance in community and little theater productions. San Fran was a great place for all of that. I loved it!"

The sparkle in Sam's eyes said even more than his words. It was the first real smile Hattie had seen. "Were you able to support yourself?" she asked, trying to sound excited.

Sam laughed. "Of course not. Not even close. Most of what I did didn't pay. But fortunately, after a couple talks, my dad agreed to send me the money each semester he would have paid for me to be in school. With the out-of-state tuition, rent, and food money I was able to make it for four more years. That had pretty much run dry in the last few months. I was living in an old two-bedroom apartment with three other guys when I got seriously sick."

"So that's why your father wanted you back here."

"I guess. I was doing okay with my friends helping me out and taking care of me at the worst times, but –"

Another coughing spell gripped Sam. He grabbed the rag from his pocket again and covered his face. It took almost two minutes to clear. It sounded awful and was difficult to watch. Hattie turned her head to conceal the tear that trickled down her cheek.

After the coughing ended, Hattie asked Sam what he would like for his meals. He professed he wasn't eating much these days, but tried to remember to take the vitamins the doctor had prescribed for him, along with the other medications he took three times a day.

He'd loaded up on all the pills before he left San Fran. As many as the doctors thought he might need to keep him as comfortable as possible, and the couple extra he begged them for. He told them the medical people on the Outer Banks wouldn't know how to treat him, and probably wouldn't want him in their offices. His doctors at the clinic hadn't disagreed with him when they'd discussed what lay ahead of him.

He informed Hattie he usually drank water, but would like a glass of orange juice in the mornings. He declined her offer of a fresh, still warm brownie, but said maybe he'd have one later.

Hattie decided that, rather than pressure him, she would just plan to make small, simple, healthy meals, like she made for her own children when they were sick, and try not to get upset if he didn't eat them. The orange juice would appear three times a day. She'd ask every now and then if he had any other special requests. That was all she could do.

When he asked, Hattie left him alone for a few minutes and unpacked his suitcases. The few clothes went in the bedroom closet and dresser, the many bottles of medications and vitamins she decided to put in the kitchen, next to the sink. She couldn't resist the temptation to look at the names of the medications, but didn't recognize any of them. Most of them had very long names.

Sam was on the porch by the time she finished unpacking his things. She sat with him for a minute before he assured her he would be fine and she could get on with the other things she had to do. They agreed she'd come back sometime after six o'clock and he'd try to eat something.

That evening, Hattie thought he looked even more drained. He didn't want anything to eat except a brownie. After he ate two bites of it, followed by a swallow of orange juice, he thanked Hattie for baking them for him, then added that he felt like it was time for an explanation.

Hattie nodded her agreement. She'd thought about little else but Sam over the last few hours; the boy she'd watched grow up, the boy she'd taught to tie his shoes and drive a car, the boy she'd loved like one of her own.

"Everything I eat goes right through me," he said. "I can't be very far from a bathroom. It's just part of this thing I have. I even have adult diapers that I have to wear if I'm going to be out for long. My dad had a private jet fly me to D.C., and fortunately there was a bathroom on it. But then the car ride here was horrible. I kept asking the driver to stop so I could go to the bathroom, but he just ignored me, except for twice. When we got to my mother's house I was a mess. I cleaned up there before we came over here."

"Is that something that's going to get better soon?" Hattie asked. She took the plate with the leftover brownie from him and sat with it in her lap.

"Afraid not." Sam shifted so he could put his feet up on the love seat. "This illness, that they don't even have a real name for, attacks the immune system so it can't fight off any viruses or bacteria that get in the body. So things just fall apart, like my digestive system, and you get every illness that comes along. I've had the flu twice in the last year, and I've got some kind of pneumonia now. I'm using this walker because I fell two weeks ago while I was in the hospital and broke my hip. But the surgeon wouldn't operate on me because a heart doctor said my heart was too weak."

"Oh, that's awful!" Hattie's face dropped and she instinctively stood and moved over to embrace him. But he held both arms up to block her.

"No, Hattie. You probably shouldn't touch me," he said, his head shaking vigorously. "That's something else about this illness. They think it's pretty contagious. The current thinking by the doctors is that it's spread through body fluids. And since I'm not planning to kiss you, have sex with you, or spit on you, you're probably safe being around me." He stopped for a couple breaths. "But, a lot of people still think it can be spread just by touching, or even by breathing the same air. I'm trying hard to cough and sneeze into a rag, but maybe you should keep your distance when I'm doing either one of those."

Hattie retreated to the chair opposite him, but landed partially on one of the arms when she sat. Once she got straightened out, she simply stared at him for a minute, trying to process what he'd said.

Neither of Sam's parents had shared this information with her. His dad probably knew all this since he'd spoken with Sam's doctors. He'd only told her Sam was very sick, had been in the hospital a couple of times, was dealing with a serious bout of pneumonia, and needed someone to take care of him. She figured his mother possibly didn't know how sick her son was. And, even if she did, Hattie knew she wouldn't speak of it to anybody. Even to the person who'd taken care of her at her worst times.

Before she could figure out what to say, Sam added, "And, if you're going to be doing my laundry, you should be wearing gloves when you touch my stuff, especially these rags." He pulled the white rag from his pocket and coughed deeply into it.

"I . . . I guess you're right," Hattie said. She had two pair of white cotton gloves at home. She figured they'd do. There was no washing machine here, so she'd carry his clothes home with her and do them there every few days. She could throw the gloves in the wash after putting Sam's clothes in.

"Please, Hattie," Sam said, his eyes reading her face, and his voice pleading with kindness. "I'm not trying to scare you. I'm just trying to . . . protect you . . . and be responsible. It would kill me if you got this thing. Or any of your family."

"Thank you," Hattie finally said. Her brain was still struggling to grasp the craziness of Sam's illness.

Apparently ready to change the topic, Sam said, "And speaking of family, how's Ben? You know I always liked it when he came over with you when I was little. Then in high school we were good friends."

"Oh, he's fine," Hattie said, thankful to be yanked out of her own thoughts. "He went in the Navy after high school, but he's back home now. He cooks at Martha's Café. 'Bout the only place he could find a job after he got home."

"That's good." Sam coughed, this time a semi-dry hack. "Would you tell him I'd like to see him? I thought maybe if some people came to see me we could sit on the front porch and talk. That way they could keep some distance from me and be out in the fresh air. He's one of the few people I'd really like to see."

"I'll do that," Hattie said. "I know he wants to see you, too." He'd said as much when she'd told him Sam was coming home. She debated for a moment how much she'd tell him about Sam's illness. She figured he should know something before he came over.

"You can tell him whatever you want about me," Sam said, as if he was reading her mind. "It'll probably come up, and I'll tell him when he gets here."

Hattie smiled. And Sam nodded.

The next morning when Hattie arrived at 8:25, Sam was still in bed. She tried to be quiet, then thought, somewhat fearfully, maybe she should check on him. His comment yesterday about no guarantee he wouldn't die tomorrow still resonated inside her. She didn't want to believe he was considering suicide, but then, she wasn't in his shoes. However, just a few seconds later she heard him say, "I'll be out in a few."

When he made it out 15 minutes later, he was wearing a lime green tee shirt with a rainbow and the words, "And Proud" emblazoned on it. Hattie was shocked at the bruises on both arms. His eyes were watching her's.

"Yeah," he said, "that's part of it. I've got them other places too." He made his way to the kitchen, and as Hattie watched he swallowed what seemed like at least eight or ten pills, with a sip of water with each one, or two. He had a brief coughing, and then choking, spell, after the last one. Hattie was afraid he was going to throw them all back up. He didn't, but looked sheepish after it was over. With the aid of the walker, he made it to the love seat.

He took only a few bites of the toast with grape jelly he agreed to try, but did drink the orange juice. When he finished, he pointed to the telephone on the cabinet beside the television.

"Is there any way you could get a longer cord for that phone?" he asked. "I'd like to take it back to the bedroom, since I'll probably be spending most of my time back there, and I want to keep in touch with a few friends back in San Fran. I didn't see an outlet for the phone in there."

"I think I can do that," Hattie said. She knew she had one somewhere at home, left over from when she had three children at home and the phone got moved between their two rooms.

"Thanks," Sam said. "I know my mom won't be happy about me running up the long-distance bill, but I've got to be able to talk to my friends. I already miss them."

"Of course you do," Hattie said. That reminded her. "Oh, Ben said to tell you he'd come by after he gets off work this evening. Should be around 7:30 or so."

"That'll be great." Sam faded away for a moment. When he came back he said, "Hattie, have you ever been to San Francisco?"

"No, never had the pleasure." She'd never been out of North Carolina, except for those two trips to Norfolk to see a specialist doctor.

"Well, it's a great place. It's like a different world from Kinnakeet. Couldn't be more different. Here, the place is dead about eight months out of the year." As Hattie watched he moved back in time and space. "Everything there is so alive. All the time. The Fillmore, the Castro, especially the Tenderloin district. It's like a major arts center for the whole West Coast. Interesting people, lots of immigrants, so lots of new foods and interesting little stores where you can buy anything and everything. Of course, I missed the heyday of the Haight-Ashbury, but I caught the last dying breaths of disco." He pulled back to the room for a second. "Have you ever heard of electronic dance music?"

Hattie shook her head. "No, never have."

He closed his eyes for a moment and was gone again. "Well, it came right after disco died. All the clubs went to it. So alive! The sounds, the beat, the synthesizers, the strobe lights. It's like disco, hip-hop, and electro-funk all came together to give birth to this incredible dance music."

Hattie could see the strain melting from his face.

"Some of my friends and I would go to the clubs to dance, and after a while we'd get to know the DJs. They knew the songs that were our favorites, so they'd announce us. 'Ladies and gentlemen, please make a little room for the D'Boys.' That was us, the Dancin' Boys, and people would make space for us on the dance floor and we'd do our thing. It was like heaven. For the next 10 minutes or so, I'd be in this . . . kind of an altered state. It was . . . just . . ." His eyes were closed again and his head tilted back, "Better than any sex I ever had."

After a few seconds of bliss, he came back to the room and looked, a bit self-consciously, at Hattie. "Sorry," he mumbled. She shook her head and gave him a little approving smile and wave.

"I bet you've never heard of the San Francisco Gay Men's Chorus" he said.

"You're right. I haven't."

"Too bad. Probably no one here has. They are this amazing chorus that has over a hundred members. They did a U.S. tour with sold-out audiences everywhere they went and standing ovations after every number. After they got back, they did a lot of free concerts around the area, and the D'Boys worked out these routines to do with three of their songs. We'd always take the space right in front of the stand, or whatever they were performing on, and we'd do this kind of interpretive dance thing. The crowds loved us, and the guys in the chorus loved us. It was . . . just incredible."

Hattie thought she saw a tear working its way down his left cheek, but just then another coughing spell took over and occupied the next couple minutes. When it cleared, Sam worked for a few seconds to get his breath, then announced he needed to go back to bed. As Hattie watched, he got to his feet, walked slowly down the narrow hall, and pushed his way into the bathroom instead of the bedroom. She told him she'd be back around noon, and slipped out the door.

When she came back at 12:15 Sam was still in bed. She made a quick decision to check on him when he didn't respond to her call, and found him laying with his head slightly elevated on his folded-over pillow. His face had a hot and drowsy look. He was sweating profusely, and using his white rag to wipe his face. He asked Hattie to get him a cold, wet washcloth, after explaining he often had what they called "night sweats" whenever he slept. The fatigue he had when he tried to do just about anything made him need to sleep, but then his sleep was fitful, at best.

Sam ate next to nothing the rest of the day. He declined any lunch, but did drink the large glass of orange juice Hattie brought to his bed. He sipped a little chicken noodle soup at dinner time, at the small kitchen table, followed by a brownie. Afterwards, Hattie asked him if he'd drink a chocolate fudge milkshake if she made him one. It was another favorite she'd made when he was a kid. He said, "Not tonight, maybe tomorrow." She plugged in the telephone cord she brought with her and set the phone beside his bed. Before she left, she reminded him of Ben's visit at 7:30.

When Ben arrived, Sam was on the front porch. He fended off the hug Ben was going to give him, then took a couple minutes to provide an abbreviated medical report to explain his action, before asking Ben to catch him up with his life. He did so, and both actively enjoyed the ensuing conversation. The visit was cut a little short when Sam announced after about 15 minutes he needed to use the bathroom and might be a while. Ben took this as his exit cue, and left after telling Sam he'd be back in a few days. Before he left, he held the front door open for Sam while he, and the walker, made their way through.

Sam had another front porch visitor the next day. The same man returned the following afternoon with two women. The first visit lasted 25 minutes, while the second one took only 10. Hattie arrived at 4:50, just as the trio was leaving. Sam offered no introduction, nor explanation.

After Hattie helped him back into the living room, he sat on the love seat and said he was going to try to stay up for a while. He asked how much the area had changed in the five years he'd been gone.

"Not much, in most ways," Hattie said. "But, there's been some more houses built along the beach. Almost all of them are huge places."

"So my parents' house isn't the biggest on the beach anymore?" he said with a weak grin.

"Lordy, no! It surely isn't," Hattie said, smiling and shaking her head at the same time. "It looks like some of them have six, maybe even seven bedrooms. And a lot of them's got swimming pools, too. Can you imagine that? A swimming pool at a house right next to the beach!"

Sam shook his head. "Some people just have too much money." Then he began to struggle to his feet and said, "Gotta' get to the bathroom." He was coughing that deep awful cough by the time he got to the door. Each coughing spell felt like a dart to Hattie's heart.

He declined anything to eat after returning to the living room, and was back in the bedroom after just a few more minutes. Hattie walked back to her house and called Sam's father. He wasn't available, but returned the call later in the evening. After listening to Hattie's report, he said he'd try to make it down to see his son within the week. Hattie urged, "Sooner is better than later."

They fell into a pattern of Hattie showing up three times a day to offer a meal. He refused anything more than a cup of apple sauce or a bowl of soup with a couple saltines. Once he drank half a milkshake. He ate two more brownies over the next three days. Hattie's visits became briefer as he spent most of his time in bed, and seemed less and less interested, or able, to engage in conversation.

Despite her promise to herself that she wouldn't give in to her feelings, Hattie's walks home were almost always tearful ones. On the walks back to his house, she talked to herself about her duty to Sam to be as upbeat and positive as she could. It was difficult, with what she had to witness each visit, but she was that kind of person, and wouldn't step inside the door until she had things right in her head, and her heart.

Sam did make it to the porch for a brief visit with a man he described as a high school teacher that he'd always liked. Several times, in the afternoons, Hattie heard him on the telephone. She guessed he spent a good amount of his waking hours talking to friends in San Francisco.

Over a bowl of soup one evening, he told her one of his friends had just died from "the illness," and another had recently been diagnosed and was in the hospital. This prompted Hattie to ask if maybe he shouldn't be in a hospital since he was obviously getting weaker with each passing day. She was pretty sure she knew what his answer was going to be, but felt she should ask.

"No. Absolutely not," he declared. "I can't go back to the hospital. First of all, I can't think of a worse place to be. Or die. I'd have to be in isolation and no one could come see me. Secondly, the only hospital on the Outer Banks wouldn't take me since they don't have an isolation unit or someone who knows about this disease. They'd just ship me out to a bigger hospital. And who knows where that'd be once they heard my diagnosis? Thirdly, I couldn't call my friends and keep in touch with them. I'd be lost without that. And . . . I'd lose you. That would be terrible."

Hattie appreciated the thought and quickly realized she couldn't argue with his points. She knew others, especially his mother, who hadn't come to visit, and had asked about him only the first of the two afternoons Hattie spent at her house cooking and cleaning, would insist he be hospitalized. As difficult as it was to watch the struggle of his breathing, and the increasingly frequent coughing that wracked his whole body, Hattie understood how he felt. She worked every day to force herself to accept he was going to do nothing further to prolong his life.

On the seventh day, while Sam was drinking his morning orange juice during a brief visit to the living room, Hattie, wearing her gloves, gathered his laundry from the pile in the corner of the bedroom. He'd been wearing only sweatpants and a tee shirt since the first day. The pants were always the same, but he put on a different tee shirt each day. She noticed there was only one pair of underwear in the pile. In the bathroom there were numerous soiled "diapers" stuffed into the trash can, making the air in the room beyond pungent. She'd been emptying the trash every other day, but today there were maybe twice as many diapers as in the past. Several washcloths and towels were ready to be washed.

She stripped the bed of the sheets and pillowcases, still damp with his sweat from the night before. She'd been doing this every other day as well. There were no other linens in the house when she'd searched the day after Sam arrived, so she'd been supplying him with fresh sets that she brought from home.

That evening, after days of debate, Hattie asked Sam, "Would you like to talk to a minister? Would that maybe be of some comfort to you?"

He turned his weary eyes on her. "No. I appreciate the thought, Hattie, but I don't feel like I'm particularly in God's good graces right now. He wouldn't like some of the thoughts I've been thinking." He drifted for a moment. "There was a church, in San Fran, that some of us went to. They welcomed us just like everybody else. Not a real denomination, like Baptist or Methodist, but just a community church were people went to worship God as they saw fit. It was really nice." He coughed for a minute. "I don't think there's a single minister here in Kinnakeet that would know what to say to me. But . . . thanks anyway."

Hattie wanted to argue with him. To point out that all God's children . . . Then she stopped. She wasn't sure even Reverend Mason, who had provided comfort to her, and probably dozens of others who were facing the end of their time on earth and preparing to join their heavenly father, would want to pay a visit to Sam. She hoped she was wrong, but decided she'd never know because she wasn't going to mention it to him.

There was no further discussion of Sam's illness or mention of his dying. Hattie watched in silent horror as his face became increasingly gaunt by the day, and his movements, especially efforts to walk, became more labored. Despite her pledge to herself not to do so, she asked him at each mealtime to try to eat a little something, and brought from home a variety of deserts and sweets that she would normally be loath to feed to her husband or children. He could not be tempted.

Two days later, she returned home from another disheartening noon visit, during which, for the second day in a row, Sam had declined to get out of bed and barely said a word. Over lunch, Herbert showed her an article in a magazine about the growing epidemic of a collection of illnesses that was being called by some the "gay cancer." Clusters of it were popping up in major cities such as New York and San Francisco. There was no known cure, and continued spread among the gay community was expected. The few details provided of the deadly symptoms sounded much too familiar.

When she finished reading, Hattie broke down into tears. As Herbert held her and comforted her, she ached to be able to do the same for Sam. She couldn't imagine going through what Sam was without someone to provide basic human contact. She hoped his friends were offering him everything else, but he couldn't see them or touch them. To her, that was at least equally important.

That evening, when she went to offer Sam supper, he was in bed. He barely acknowledged her when she knocked on the door and slipped into his room. After a moment of looking at his emaciated face, she slipped on the pair of white gloves she brought with her, then, almost immediately, pulled them off and threw them on the floor. She slid the sheet off his body, and climbed into the bed beside him. A moment later she had his naked body wrapped in her arms.

Sam opened his eyes for just a moment and murmured, "Oh, Miss Hattie. Thank you." Then, a second later said, "It's time."

She whispered back, "I love you."

A minute later he passed away.

Sam's funeral was attended only by his parents, Hattie, Herbert, Ben, and the high school teacher.

The next day, Hattie got a letter in the mail from Platt and Platt, Attorneys at Law, advising her that Sam had left her the house in his will. The letter requested she come to the office to sign some papers.

Sons And Daughters

"Welcome to Open Book from WMEP, Maine Public Radio. This is Kathy Dawson, and today with me on Open Book are Tom and Ginny Nesmith. They're a married couple who've recently published a book describing a remarkable and very historically important experience during their voyage on a small sailboat from Rockport, Maine down the coast to Melbourne, Florida and back. The book is entitled, *Sons and Daughters: A True American Story*. It's already making its way rapidly up the best seller charts. Welcome Tom and Ginny."

"Thank you, Kathy. We're happy to be here." Ginny smiled as she pulled her chair closer to the microphone.

Tom offered a quick, "Yes we are. Thank you for having us."

"Well, I've read your book and I must say it's fascinating. I understand all the attention you and the book are getting. But to set the stage for this remarkable story, you actually built the sailboat over the course of three years in a big garage at your home right here in Rockport, if I have that right."

"Yes," Ginny said, "That's right. It's a 35-footer and Tom did about 90-percent of the work. I helped out when and where I could. He's quite the craftsman."

"And this was the first major trip on the boat," Kathy said.

"It was," Tom replied. "We made a few small day trips ahead of time and got all, well, most, of the kinks worked out. The boat served us well on the trip."

"With a trip like that you need to be able to know and trust your vessel, I'm sure." Kathy peeked at her notes, sitting beside a copy of the book in front of her. "In the introduction to your book you give the readers a little background about building the boat and the trip you planned sailing down the coast. Can you tell us a little bit about that?"

Tom leaned into his microphone. "Yes. We decided before the trip that we'd each keep a journal, then when we returned we'd try to put together something that would tell the story of our sailing adventure. We planned to write about some of our experiences at sea and some of the interesting things that happened at our ports of call, including stories about the people we met along the way."

Kathy nodded. "But then one particular experience you had changed the entire focus of what you would end up writing about, and gave us the gift of this wonderful book. It's absolutely one of the most interesting books I've read in a long time. I know everyone out there listening to us will want to get a copy of your book when they hear what happened." Kathy offered a sincere smile and nodded again toward her guests. "Would you tell our listeners what began with that dark and stormy night off the coast of North Carolina?"

"Will do," Tom said. He shifted in his seat and took a sip of water.

"We were well over half-way through the trip down to Florida, off the coast of North Carolina, as you said. The radar showed a rapidly moving storm coming up the coast and we knew we needed to get somewhere safe. We hoped to get to Hatteras and into the harbor there for the night. We were racing both the darkness and the storm. By the time we got within a few miles of Hatteras nightfall was rapidly approaching and the wind was nearing gale force. We'd heard all the stories about the Graveyard of the Atlantic and Diamond Shoals off the coast there, and were desperately hoping we weren't going to have to make a mayday call to the Coast Guard and end up another boat at the bottom of the ocean."

"I bet things were pretty tense, for both of you," Kathy said.

"Oh, they were!" Ginny said. "We'd taken down the sails, battened down the hatches, and were praying that our little motor had enough juice to get us around the point and into the harbor at Hatteras."

"And I understand it did."

"Barely," Tom said. "But the wind was so fierce, even once we got into the sound and close to Hatteras, we couldn't get into the harbor there. We were blown on up the inside of the Pamlico sound. Finally, we saw some lights off to starboard and figured we'd try to find a place to tie up there."

"And then you saw something else."

"Yes," Ginny said, after glancing at Tom for a second. "There was a light. What looked like a high-powered flashlight, shining at us from the shore off our starboard bow. It was moving. It would shine right at us, then shine on the water between us and the shore, almost like the person holding it was beckoning us, or signaling us, a path to come ashore. We made a quick decision to try to do just that. We were barely able to make it, with the wind trying to blow us farther on up the sound, but we followed the light and found ourselves in a little harbor. Two of the five boat slips were empty, and the guy with the flashlight guided us right into one of them. Tom tossed him a rope and he tied us up. Against the wind he shouted, *Welcome to Kinnakeet.*"

"And I bet you were glad to be there," Kathy said.

"Oh yeah," Ginny said. "We would be glad to be anywhere off the water, at that point."

"And tell us what happened then."

"The man shouted his name," Tom said. "It sounded like 'Scar' or 'Tar,' or something like that. He said we should grab our bags and follow him. We were hoping to find a motel, some place with a hot shower and a comfortable bed. We would have settled for a hot shower and slept on the floor at that point. Mind you, the rain is seconds away and it's nearly pitch dark at 6:30 p.m. We had little choice, so we grabbed our overnight duffel bag, did a quick check to secure the boat, and he helped us up on the deck, giving us a strong grip to keep us from getting blown into the water. I gave him our names. He nodded and led the way to the street with his flashlight. We followed him, with some difficulty because of the wind, to a house on the second street back from the harbor. About 30 seconds before we got there, all heck broke loose, and the rain came in torrents."

"And I bet you were feeling . . ."

"Rescued, is probably the best word," Ginny said. "We were just going to ask him where we could find a motel, but so far we hadn't been able to talk to him. I was thinking once we were in the house, and out of the storm, we could catch our breath, thank him for his help, and maybe he would drive us to a motel. But that's not what happened."

"What happened is a lot more interesting than that," Kathy said. She motioned to Ginny and Tom with her index finger. "But it's time for us to take a break. When we come back our listeners will be amazed at what transpires next. We'll be right back."

Kathy nodded to the engineer in the next booth, then said, "This is being recorded, as you know, so this break is just to give you two a chance to relax for a moment. The crew will insert a couple minutes of NPR acknowledgments and begging." The couple nodded at her, appreciating the honesty.

"You're doing great. Both of you. I know what's coming from reading the book, but I can't wait to hear you describe it." She took a look at the digital timer on the wall. "We've got about 18 minutes left, and we'll take one more break. So tell as much as you want to. You can leave the audience hanging, if you'd like. Make them buy the book to find out some of the more fascinating details. I'll plug the book before we wrap."

Tom and Ginny took a few seconds to stand and stretch. After a minute, Tom put his hand on Ginny's shoulder. "You just keep going and finish out the story. It's really your story."

Ginny nodded and swallowed a sip of water. They both took their seats. Ginny nestled up to the microphone while Tom sat back in his chair.

"Welcome back, folks. We're here with Tom and Ginny Nesmith, and we're talking about their book, *Sons and Daughters: A True American Story.* They were telling us about getting through a dangerous storm into the tiny harbor at Kinnakeet, North Carolina and the man who guided them in there, then took them to his home. Do you want to pick it up from there, Ginny?"

"Yes. Well, from what we could see of the front of the house in the storm, it was an old, single story house with aged cedar shake siding. So close to the sound, we wondered if it was in the flood zone, but Scar assured us later this storm wasn't going to flood much of anything. It was expected to move through overnight, and didn't even have a name."

Kathy raised her index finger. "For our listeners who don't live near the coast, if a storm doesn't have a name . . ."

"That means it's not a hurricane or a tropical storm." Tom said. "Other storms can cause some flooding and wind damage along the coast, but most coastal communities, like Kinnakeet, are pretty used to them and take them in stride."

"Okay. Now what happened when you got in the house?"

Ginny continued the story. "We got our first good look at him as he peeled out of his old yellow slicker and bucket hat. He was short, thin, probably 70-something-years-old. His face had a large scar from the edge of his right eye down to his jaw, so we understood his name was Scar. His skin was dark and splotchy, like he'd been in the weather his whole life. What little hair he had was white. Shortly after we got in the door, he pointed us to the bathroom and told us to dry off and come to the kitchen when we were ready. He was going to start preparing dinner.

"There'd been no mention of dinner, or anything else at this point. He just assumed we were hungry, which we were, and he was going to feed us. We were grateful, and when we came out he had a big pot of clam chowder on the stove and was making grilled cheese sandwiches. The kitchen was delightfully warm and smelled . . . like clam chowder. The New England kind. The type we were used to. It was a bit awkward, but we stood at the small kitchen table and started to tell him how much we appreciated his help getting into the harbor. I asked him how he knew there was a boat out in the sound needing help."

"What'd he say?" Kathy asked.

"He said, *I had a dream you were coming.*" Ginny paused to watch Kathy's nod, then continued.

"Tom and I looked at each other, but decided to let that pass. So, I asked him where we could find a motel. He said something to the effect of, *Nonsense. You're staying here tonight.* I wasn't sure, but I'd have bet a thousand dollars this little place had only one bedroom. We tried to argue with him, but he just said, *Sit down. Dinner's about ready.* So we did, and had the best dinner we'd had since we left home, topped off with a piece of fig cake, which he described as a Kinnakeet specialty."

"So, how were you feeling about this man at this point?" Kathy asked, looking at Ginny, then Tom. "Sounds like there's some strange things going on."

Tom leaned into his microphone. "I was getting a weird vibe. I mean, he seemed like a nice old man at first, just trying to help us out. But, some seemingly nice old guys aren't so nice. My grandfather was one of those. And this guy was a bit peculiar. Telling us he knew we were out there in the storm from a dream. Come on! He couldn't have seen us. Or heard us. And insisting we stay for dinner, and stay the night? I was ready to grab Ginny and head out the door and start walking. I thought we'd be safer spending the night on the boat, rocking and tossing all night."

Kathy grinned. "And you, Ginny, how were you feeling?"

"I had a different vibe," Ginny said without a moment's hesitation. "I liked the guy from the moment I saw him standing on the dock. I wasn't sure why."

"Interesting. So, pick it up there. What happened next?"

"Tom and I started asking him questions over dinner. He deflected the questions about himself initially and talked instead about the village, Kinnakeet. He gave us a history lesson about its long history as a Native American village, then a fishing and boat building settlement once the Anglos came. And how now it's largely a summer vacation community.

"Then he asked us what we knew of our family lineage. I thought that was a strange question, but I told him I'd traced my family line back six generations and actually had some relatives who lived in eastern North Carolina. Tom told him what little he knew of his family history, and their roots in New England. Scar told us that he was of coastal North Carolina Native American lineage. His family had kept their bloodline pure, not intermarrying with Anglos until the early 1900s. Thus, he was one-fourth Native American. His grandfather and father both worked on fishing boats. He'd spent his whole life in Kinnakeet, except for a few years in the Navy, where he'd gotten the scar on his face.

"Then, about the time we were finishing dinner, he said something really odd. Out of the blue he said, *You know, Ginny, it's no accident you're here.*"

"That must have caught you off guard."

"Oh yeah. It really did. Then the next thing he said was, *I have something for you, Ginny. Something very important.*"

"And you were thinking . . ."

Ginny paused for just a second. "I was thinking how could this strange man, who I'd just met, in this little village in North Carolina, almost 1,000 miles away from home, possibly have something important to give me."

"Sounds about right," Kathy said.

"But then he said . . ."

The Gods have brought us together to fulfill a mission. But right now the two of you need to get cleaned up and get some sleep. I imagine you'll want to get up early and get underway. I'll fix breakfast and explain everything in the morning.

"And at that point you had no idea what he was talking about."

"Right," Ginny said. "We couldn't imagine what kind of mission this man could possibly be on that involved me." She looked to Tom who picked up the story.

"So then he got us some fresh towels and washcloths, and while we were taking showers he put clean sheets on the bed. We were right, there was only one bedroom, but he insisted we take it and he'd sleep on the sofa. The storm was raging outside and we didn't really feel like we had any options, so we did what he said. I don't know if Ginny got any sleep that night –"

"Not much, between the storm and wondering what Scar had in store for us in the morning," Ginny said.

"Well, I got a little," Tom continued. "At 5:30 in the morning, Scar had coffee and freshly baked blueberry muffins ready for us, which were delicious, by the way. After we ate, he told us to stay where we were. Then he cleared the table, settled in his chair, and began with his story.

In 1587 a group of colonists from England landed in the harbor at Roanoke Island, just a few miles north of here. The colonists set up a small village, with the help of the Native Americans, who greeted them warmly. The first child born in the new colony was named Virginia Dare. She was the granddaughter of the commander of the group, Governor John White. During the fall of 1587, John White and a crew sailed back to England, planning to return before Christmas with supplies for the colony. Because of a war between England and Spain he was unable to return for three years. When he came back in 1590 the colonists were gone.

"He asked if we'd heard this story. I told him I had and Ginny said she had too, and wasn't that called the Lost Colony story? He scoffed at this, and said the colony wasn't lost, and that myth was made up by a playwright in the 1930s and continued to be promoted so the play with this name, performed every summer on Roanoke Island, could be commercially successful. Then he continued."

When John White returned he met some of the Natives of the friendly tribe that he'd known before he left. They told him the colony had moved to Croatoan, the place we now call Hatteras Island. Indeed, the word Croatoan was found carved in a tree at the colony site as John White had instructed them to do if they moved elsewhere. John White knew of Croatoan, had been there, and tried to set sail to rejoin his family and deliver the supplies. But a bad storm and a near mutiny of the crew, who were desperate to return home, prevented this. He reluctantly sailed back to England, never to return. One of the Natives he talked with before returning to England was my ancestor.

"How fascinating," Kathy said waving her hand at the engineer's booth. "You were talking to a descendant of one of the people present at the founding of America's first English colony. But, let's stop there and take a quick break. When we come right back we'll hear the rest of Tom and Ginny's amazing story. Don't go away."

When the engineer gave the all clear, Kathy said, "You're great story tellers. Sales of your book are going to skyrocket even more when this airs next week. You need to be prepared. Let's take about a minute break, then do our last few minutes."

Everyone stood for a quick stretch. Then Tom moved to Ginny with his arms out and she stepped into his hug. They were still wrapped around each other when Kathy said, "All right you two. Break it up. Let's get back on the air." Tom and Ginny smiled at each other, then Kathy, and resumed their seats.

Kathy nodded to the engineer. "We're back with Tom and Ginny Nesmith and a fascinating account of a happening in North Carolina from their best-selling book, *Sons and Daughters: A True American Story*. Tom and Ginny, you've got us all glued to our radios and headsets. Please tell us what happened next with Scar."

Ginny gave a quick nod. "Scar said that where exactly on Croatoan, or Hatteras Island, the colony settled has remained unclear through the ages. The best guess was around what is now the towns of Buxton and Frisco, but another possibility was Kinnakeet, which for the Natives was a well-known gathering place and wide spot on the narrow Hatteras Island. Scar then said . . ."

Before he left to return to England, John White gave my ancestor a pendant that he'd brought with him to give to his granddaughter, Virginia Dare. He asked that if his daughter, Eleanor, or granddaughter, Virginia, should return, or could be found on Croatoan, that he give the pendant to them. My ancestor pledged to do this. He stayed on Roanoke Island for many years, then began to search Croatoan for the white mother and child. He was told several times they had been seen in the past, but had gone away. He travelled all the way to the island tip, at what is now Hatteras Village, but never located either mother or child.

When that ancestor neared his death, he passed the pendant along to his son with the instructions given to him by John White. That man never found Eleanor or Virginia and passed the pendant to his son, and he passed it to his son, and so on. Each time the pendant was passed along, the story of the pendant and the instructions were repeated. Early in the passing of the pendant one of the holders had a vision – that Virginia's descendant would return to Croatoan from far away. She would come by boat, as Virginia's mother, father, and grandfather had. She wouldn't necessarily know her heritage, but the holder of the pendant would know who she was when they met. My father told me the story of the pendant and the vision when he passed it along to me almost thirty years ago, just a year before he died.

Ginny stopped at that point and the room fell silent. Finally, Kathy could wait no longer. "And . . .?"

"And," Ginny finally said, "he told us he'd prayed many times asking what to do with the pendant since he didn't have a son. He and his wife, who'd died ten years ago, hadn't been able to have children. Each time he prayed the answer had been to be patient, that she would come. Then he said he'd had a dream two nights ago that Virginia's descendant would arrive the next day. He waited and watched the ocean through the morning and afternoon. But when the storm came up he thought she would more likely arrive via the sound than the turbulent sea. And that was why he was at the harbor with his flashlight."

"Amazing!" Kathy said. "And then he asked you one other thing, if I remember right."

"That's right. He asked me what my given first name was. At that point, of course, I was shocked. I stuttered, but told him my given name was Virginia. He asked if I had relatives with that name. Again, I was stunned when I recalled that almost every woman in my mother's family line, as far back as I'd traced it, was named Virginia. The one who didn't have a daughter had a granddaughter who was named Virginia. Unfortunately, I was the oldest living Virginia, as my mother had died the year before, and the family had been giving birth mostly to sons."

Kathy was nodding enthusiastically. "So that name really was part of the heritage for women in your family."

"Yes, it was. But no one had ever said anything, at least to me, about why. It was just a name we all loved. Apparently for some deeply buried unconscious reason."

"I was pretty shocked too," Tom said. "I was trying to doubt everything he said. Trying to believe he was making up some kind of tall tale. I was waiting for the punch line. But he was so sincere. So . . . believable."

Ginny nodded. "Yes, he really was. But then the real kicker happened. He got up from the table and went to the hall closet. He returned with a small package, wrapped in a very old piece of cotton cloth. He placed it on the table and said . . ."

This is the pendant. The holder of the pendant is only allowed to look at it when it is first given to him. I last saw it 28 years ago. Only fourteen sets of eyes have seen this pendant since 1590. It is now my honor to give it to you, Virginia.

"He pushed the package across the table to me. He had this expression of . . . relief, or maybe accomplishment. At first I didn't want to touch it, or unwrap the box. I wasn't completely convinced that it was meant for me, and couldn't really grasp that I was a descendant of Virginia Dare. I was almost afraid of it. But then, after a few seconds of sitting there stunned, a sense of calm came over me. I looked at him. He nodded and said, *Yes. It is you.* Then my hands reached out and touched the package, almost on their own. I slowly unwrapped the cloth. Inside was a small box made of very old wood. I lifted the lid off, and . . . there was the pendant."

After a moment of silence, Kathy almost whispered, "I know there are pictures of the pendant in the book, but can you describe it for our listeners?"

"Yes," Ginny said. "It was a very old silver British coin, about the size of our half dollar, with a small hole drilled through it. A small silver ring hanging through the hole was attached to a woven silver chain. On the front of the coin was the image of a woman with a crown on her head that I later learned was Queen Elizabeth the First. Her name and some other words were stamped around the edge of the coin. On the back, where there once had been a shield or coat of arms, most of the surface had been sanded or smoothed and the words 'Virginia Dare' were written in old

English printing. It was amazingly clear with little tarnish."

"And did you put it on?" Kathy asked.

"No. Not until much later. And, the first time I put it around my neck . . . well, that's described in the book."

"But you did take the pendant with you."

"Yes. We tried to argue with Scar that we should leave the pendant in his trusted hands and pick it up on the way back up the coast. But he wouldn't consider that. When I put the pendant back in the box he wrapped the cloth around it, clasped both of my hands for a couple seconds, then put the box in my right hand. He said . . ."

My job is done. The sacred task entrusted to my family over 400 years ago is accomplished. It has been an honor to meet you and do my duty . . . Now off with you. The storm is gone and the sailing is clear for the day.

"So you left Kinnakeet with the pendant in hand and went on with your sailing trip down the coast," Kathy said. "And, for our listeners' benefit, there are a lot of other fascinating facts and happenings associated with the pendant described in the book. But, one more important thing . . . You did stop back in Kinnakeet to see Scar on your way back up the coast. Would you like to tell our listeners what happened then, or would you like for them to find out when they read the book?"

Ginny and Tom looked at each other for a moment. Then Tom said, "I don't mind telling that . . . We'd obviously talked a great deal about the pendant and Scar as we sailed down the coast, during our brief stay in Florida, then back north. There were many things we wanted to ask him about his life and his ancestors. When we docked in the harbor at Kinnakeet we were excited as we walked to Scar's house. Then we were stunned when we found it in the process of being demolished."

Tom frowned and glanced at Ginny who was shaking her head. "We asked a couple of people in neighboring houses where we could find Scar. Finally, we found someone who told us that Scar had packed up and left a month ago, which would have put it just a few days after we left him. He didn't say where he was going, only that he was anxious to go home and tell his ancestors what he'd done."

"Well," Kathy said, "that certainly is an amazing experience the two of you had. Could you tell us just a little more about what you subsequently learned about the pendant, or rather the coin?"

Ginny smiled. "Yes. I had a numismatist who specializes in British coins examine it. He authenticated it as a sterling silver one shilling coin struck in the Tower Mint in London between 1587 and 1589. It has the distinctive crescent mark on it that the British mint used to identify coins produced during those years."

"Fascinating. And, may I ask where the pendant is now?"

"Yes," Ginny said. "It's locked away in a very safe place. The location of that is not revealed, or even hinted at, in the book."

"Probably a good idea. And, may I also ask . . . that pendant is, no doubt, the most valuable and historic relic of America's first English settlement. Have you considered donating it to a museum? I'm sure there are many that would love to display it, and millions of people who would love to see it in person."

Tom looked at Ginny, who nodded for him to go ahead. "We've considered donating it to the visitors center on Roanoke Island, near the location of the first colony, and where John White was when he gave it to Scar's ancestor. Or possibly the Frisco Native American Museum on Hatteras Island. But we may also pass it along to our daughter. We haven't made a decision yet. And no, you don't need to ask what our daughter's first name is."

Kathy grinned and nodded. "I was pretty sure of that. Now, anything else you'd like to add for our listeners before we wrap up?"

Ginny was quick to respond. "Yes. I'd like to say that the real heroes of this truly American story are Scar and the 14 ancestral fathers and sons who took responsibility for the pendant over the course of 431 years, and who took the request from John White as a sacred family duty. I only wish we knew more about them, and could tell more of their story, than I was able to share in the book."

Kathy reached in front of her and patted the book. "Well, again, thank both of you for sharing this wonderful story with us. Let's make sure our listeners know that among the many other details included in the book are the results of the ancestry DNA test Ginny took as soon as she got back to Maine, and some additional family genealogy work she has completed that adds greatly to our understanding of her unique heritage. There's also a great deal of insight into how the pendant, and the experience with Scar, have changed both Tom and Ginny's lives.

"I encourage all of you to go right out and buy your copy of *Sons and Daughters: A True American Story* by Tom and Ginny Nesmith. It's a great read, and a great story . . . For WMEP, Maine Public Radio, and Open Book, this is Kathy Dawson. Good day."

Captain Jack

Joko Christopoulos was called many things during the few years in the later part of his life that he spent in Kinnakeet. Among them were, "Bum," "Fraud," "Crazy Old Man," "That Ol' Drunk," and a few others. But his favorite thing to be called was "Captain Jack."

Captain Jack appeared in Kinnakeet one day around 1970 from . . . well, no one knows for sure where. His stories about his background varied from day to day and audience to audience. But he spoke with pride about being born in the small Greek fishing village of Fiskardo, and coming to America as a child.

He usually said he'd come from most recently working on a commercial fishing boat out of Wanchese. When he talked about that time, he was the captain of the boat. However, there was great skepticism among the locals about that. When inquiries were made, no one in Wanchese had ever heard of a Greek fishing boat captain there. A couple guys who worked the dock thought he may have been on the crew of the *Carolina Classic*, but weren't sure. He wouldn't say why he wasn't still working there, but problems with alcohol were suspected.

One thing Jack could do better than most was tell a story. He had a way about him that could make believers out of the most skeptical and rational of listeners. His slight accent somehow imparted a sense of plausibility, and he knew all the nautical lingo. He'd throw in a "forecastle," or "quarterdeck" when talking about a ship, and could describe the ocean currents and different types of waves that a ship captain had to be aware of and what they foretold.

According to him, he'd spent a lot of time on ships of all kind and had sailed the world. He talked with great assurance about the years he spent on freighters, frigates, and commercial fishing boats of all shapes and sizes, mostly out of ports in New England, including Philadelphia, Providence, and New York.

He claimed to have captained a four-masted schooner, the *Oceanus*, built at a shipyard in Nova Scotia as a replica of the fine vessels that plied the eastern seaboard in the 18th and 19th centuries. The ship carried well-paying passengers on recreational voyages up and down the coast, sometimes even to the Bahamas and ports in the Western Caribbean.

With little or no provocation, he would talk at great lengths about his experiences at sea, especially riding out perilous squalls, tropical storms, and even hurricanes. His fantastic stories even included one about fighting off modern-day pirates in hand-to-hand combat on one particular voyage of the schooner in the Caribbean.

By his account, the *Oceanus* was lost at sea when a rogue tropical cyclone drove her into a reef off the coast of Grand Cayman. However, the entire crew and 33 passengers were saved by his heroic efforts to get them into the lifeboats just as the ship broke apart and sank.

Jack also knew the stories of all the pirates who plied the coasts of the Carolinas and Caribbean. The details in his stories, accurate or made up, might make you think he personally knew, and maybe even served with, the likes of Blackbeard and Calico Jack, and possibly even had a personal relationship with Anne Bonny.

He also knew the tales of the many shipwrecks off the Outer Banks. Of course, by the time he came to Kinnakeet, there was a fine book detailing many of these wrecks in the Graveyard of the Atlantic. It was assumed, by locals in the know, that he'd purchased the book and memorized a few of these stories, right down to the details of distress signals sent and the heroics of the lifesaving crews.

His favorite shipwreck story to tell was of the *Carroll A. Deering*, which was found mysteriously abandoned, under full sail, on Diamond Shoals off Cape Hatteras in 1921. He claimed to know exactly what happened to the captain and crew of the ship on its way back home from Rio de Janeiro. His tale was a highly detailed one of conflict between the captain and first mate throughout the voyage, leading to outright mutiny and murder. His claimed source for his "facts" was a weathered old seaman he had befriended as a younger man, who claimed to be a survivor of the mutiny, and a couple days at sea in a lifeboat.

Jack's appearance certainly helped sell his stories.

His light brown skin had a bit of a golden undertone, and was quite weather-beaten and creased. His eyes were olive and deep. He rarely trimmed his full beard in those days, so it was always scraggly. His hair was salt and pepper – mostly salt, unkempt, and shoulder-length. He was always seen around the village wearing old black jeans, a black-and-white striped shirt, or an old white shirt with the sleeves rolled up. When the wind was up, or it was cold, he wore a bandana tied loosely around his neck, and even sometimes a beaten-up old white sailor's cap. His manner of dress, and his swagger, were right out of Hollywood central casting.

After just a week in Kinnakeet, Jack stumbled into a job as a "captain" on a small, six-passenger boat working out of the Kinnakeet harbor that took tourists out on sunset-watching or half-day fishing trips in the sound. The owner of the boat, Walter Midgett, hired Jack without much of an interview or screening process, because his previous captain up and quit one day in the middle of the summer over a dispute about pay. The job lasted until the end of the tourist season, which in those days was Labor Day weekend. Walter never said much about why he didn't hire Jack back the next year, but there were rumors.

After that summer, Jack worked a series of part-time jobs in the village. Really, anything he could find. It wasn't difficult to find work during the season, but after the tourists left, the pickings were slim. Eventually, he would get on with a painting or remodeling crew working on houses while they were empty.

It seemed Jack's place of residence changed often. In the summer, when every available apartment or rooming house was rented, Jack could often be found sleeping outside. He had a few favorite places that were cooler than others and afforded some protection from the heat and rain. In the off-season, some kind soul with a big heart (of which there were many in Kinnakeet), would allow him to stay in one of the cottages that would be vacant, often in exchange for some type of work. One year it was rumored that the widow Kane took pity on him in more ways than one, and provided him with room and board in exchange for painting her house and two rental cottages, along with other personal services.

While Jack was never known to be a panhandler, he certainly came to know the managers or owners of the grocery store and bakeries in the village, and the times that they closed in the evenings. He often showed up, always at the back door, and kindly accepted any offerings of food that might otherwise go to waste. There was no "food kitchen" or other services offered for the indigent or homeless back in those days.

His second summer in the village, Jack offered to teach Laura White, one of the generous bakery owners, how to make baklava. She thought there might be a few customers who would be interested in this, so she agreed to give it a try.

Jack gave her a list of necessary ingredients for the family recipe, then showed up at 5:30 a.m. the next Wednesday morning when she arrived at the shop, and worked with her to produce the first batch. It sold modestly over the next couple days. But the next Wednesday, when she put small samples on the counter for people to try, she sold out in the first four hours. Jack came to the shop the next two Wednesdays to help with the baking, now four pans of the delicacy instead of the original two. His "secret ingredient" was lemon zest added to the sugar, vanilla, and honey sauce that was poured over the top as the treat came out of the oven.

Laura took over baking the baklava twice a week after the first four weeks. It then became a Wednesday and Friday special. "Mama Christo's Baklava," was sold out each day by the early afternoon. No one, except the couple of customers who asked, knew the origin of their favorite indulgence.

Each Wednesday and Friday after that, during the eight months that the bakery was open during the year, Laura set aside a couple pieces for Jack. She gave them to him, along with a large bottle of water, and whatever other leftover goodies there might be, when he came in the front door just before closing time. They always shared a nice couple of minutes together while Jack savored the taste of his homeland. They became good friends.

Throughout his time in the village, Jack's supposed background and storytelling abilities provided him with some degree of notoriety. He was an occasional guest at the various civic clubs up and down the Outer Banks. He would be provided transportation, partake in a lunch, then, after the club's brief meeting, regale the attendees with his tales from the sea.

This was always with the instruction ahead of time that his storytelling would be limited to one specific topic, such as the coastal shipwrecks, the story of the *Carroll A. Deering,* or life at sea on the *Oceanus*, in order to stay within the 20- minute time frame made available. However, over the couple of years that Jack had these opportunities, his stories got longer, wilder, and generally less constrained. His language was also known to more frequently cross the line of good taste. Eventually the invitations dried up.

At the same time, Jack was a frequent speaker at the area elementary and secondary schools. He especially loved to go to the schools in Hatteras and, dressed in what he called his "pirate get-up," tell wild tales of pirate adventures off the nearby coast. The volume of his voice would go up and down as he described the pitch of the deck of the poor merchant ships as the crew tried to battle off the hoard of pirates storming on board, armed with muskets and sabers. He'd pace up and down, and his hands and arms would wave wildly, like the skull and crossbones banner whipping in the wind from a pirate galleon.

The children loved him and his stories. The teachers and administrators not as much. Just like the talks to the civic groups, his tales became more "exciting" over the years. The adults thought his stories of beheadings and walking the plank were a bit too graphic for the young audience. They also found his language was sometimes a bit too "salty." So, like all good things, his appearances at the schools came to an end.

Jack had a number of acquaintances in Kinnakeet, but not a lot of friends. He was pleasant enough to everybody, but was seen by most of the locals as a "character" to be tolerated, and often talked about. But someone in his small group of friends talked him into going to an Alcoholics Anonymous meeting.

The closest meetings back then were in Hatteras, with Nags Head being the next option. One of his friends would pick him up and give him a ride to a meeting, as Jack didn't have a car, or a driver's license. Some doubted whether he'd ever held a captain's license to operate a boat either.

He had a hard time adjusting initially to the A.A. environment. Talking about himself wasn't a problem, but opening up about his troubles with alcohol was. He had to be gently redirected at meetings to focus on the negative effects of his drinking, rather than tell tales of the endless barrels of rum he could smuggle into the States from the Caribbean aboard the *Oceanus*, or nights spent in glorious drunken frenzy prowling the bars and taverns in exotic ports of call. He would listen attentively to the stories of the other attendees, but it wasn't until his fifth meeting that he was willing to declare, "I'm Jack, and I'm an alcoholic."

Jack was extremely fortunate that he had the strong support of the A.A. meetings, and the equally important backing of the Kinnakeet A.A. community. This group, of men and women, took him in and made sure his basic needs were met, in addition to any kind of assistance he needed to stay away from the demon rum. Allen Hopkins became his sponsor, but Jack was never one to earnestly work the steps.

His housing was more stable from the time he started attending meetings, as was his employment. This was mostly due to the generosity of his A.A. friends. As time moved on, he was an occasional guest at the dinner table of these families, who allowed him to tell his tales over the meal, within the bounds of sobriety.

Like many alcoholics before him, and since, Jack had an occasional slip. He would get his hands on the better part of a 12-pack of beer, or a bottle or two of cheap wine, typically courtesy of the village youth, or some partying summer tourists, who would pay him with the alcohol for an evening of tall tales. At those times, he could usually be found the next morning at one of his old sleeping spots from his homeless days, too hungover and embarrassed to go near the quarters supplied to him by his A.A. friends. He would always get back on the wagon the next day, with sincere apologies to his local support system, and a full confession at the next A.A. meeting.

Allen decided one warm day in May to see if Jack would like to go for a boat ride. His plan was to take him out in the sound on his 21-foot sport boat and after a couple minutes, turn the controls over to him. He wanted to do this, half out of a desire to let Jack, at least to a slight degree, experience the thrill of being back on the water again, and half just to see if Jack knew what he was doing at the helm.

Jack readily accepted the offer, and was obviously very excited. He was working on a remodeling project for Allen at the time, and, in addition to some time back on the water, a few hours away from work would be welcome.

A bit to Allen's surprise, Jack showed that he absolutely knew what he was doing with just a minute's orientation on the controls. He simply glowed while putting the boat through its paces in the deeper sections of the sound, and briefly out in the ocean at Hatteras. For much of the time, he couldn't stop talking, bringing up some newer versions of a few of the old tales. He insisted on showing Allen one of the "honey holes" where he used to take fishermen on their half-day outings. Allen broke out a couple fishing rods, and they spent a delightful hour spin casting downwind to red drum, boating seven of them. Over the next couple days, Allen spread the news of Jack's boat handling skills.

It was two months later that Jack gave his last, and probably his best, story-telling performance in Kinnakeet.

He met Paul Theiss outside the grocery store late on a Saturday afternoon. Paul was smoking a cigarette while his wife finished up the initial food shopping for the family's week-long stay. The nanny was caring for the three children back at the rented house.

After listening for just a couple minutes to Jack's introductory seafaring tales, which were part of his greeting of new acquaintances, Paul informed Jack that he was from the Chesapeake Bay area of Maryland. He'd spent a good deal of time on the water while growing up, and was involved in a family fishing business. He'd always been fascinated by stories of pirates and shipwrecks, and that was one of the reasons he wanted to bring his family to the Outer Banks. He was looking forward to sharing his interest in these topics with his wife and children while "on location."

He asked Jack if he would be interested in joining his family for a picnic lunch the next day and share some of his stories with them. Of course, Jack was delighted to be asked, and gave Paul directions to the little village park just a couple blocks from the harbor.

Captain Jack was in his element that day. He was stone, cold sober, and wearing freshly laundered clothes. He'd tidied up his beard, and made an effort to cut his hair, or at least trim around the edges. He greeted the Mrs., children, and nanny with courtesy and restraint.

He engaged in polite conversation leading up to lunch, making a point to ask the children about their morning on the beach and their impression of Kinnakeet. He agreed with them that there certainly wasn't much else to do around there besides the beach, but, knowing their dad's interest, encouraged visits to the Bodie Island, Manteo, and Hatteras lighthouses.

After the lunch of sandwiches, chips, cookies, and iced tea, he eagerly launched into storytelling mode. It felt like the best of the old times to him, as he entertained the family without pre-arranged limits on his time or tales. As the family sat on a picnic table, he started out with highlights of his time captaining the *Oceanus* and his other exploits at sea, but before long he was cavorting in front of them, telling and acting out his tales of pirates and shipwrecks.

The children, for that matter the whole family, were enthralled. The little ones interrupted occasionally to ask a question, but for the most part sat wide-eyed and tuned in. Mr. and Mrs. Theiss, and the nanny as well, showed their obvious pleasure with frequent smiles, nods, and other expressions of delight as they watched the children enjoy the performance. A young couple, who was walking by, even stopped for a few minutes to listen. They gave him a smiling nod and wave when they moved on.

Jack had decided ahead of time to end with the ghost ship story of the *Carroll A. Deering*, and his knowledge of the true fate of its crew. When he started this tale, over an hour into his presentation, Mr. Theiss momentarily gasped and grabbed the picnic table in front of him. He stared intently at Jack as the story unwound and the tale of mutiny and murder came to life.

When Jack finished this final story, the family gave him a rousing ovation. He acknowledged this with a curt bow, then took a seat and a sip of tea. Mr. Theiss rose immediately and approached Jack. He asked him to walk with him for a moment, while his wife and the nanny put the remains of the lunch away and gathered the children to head back to the house.

As Jack relayed the story to Allen the next day, Mr. Theiss told him that his maternal great-grandfather, Gardiner Deering, owned the shipping company that built and owned the *Carroll A. Deering*. The ship was named after his youngest son – the company bookkeeper, and Mr. Theiss's grandfather. It was the last ship built by the Deering Company, and was one of the last commercial wooden sailing ships built anywhere in the world.

Mr. Theiss was fascinated with the version Jack told of the ship's demise and his source of information. On the spot, he asked Jack if he would come back with him to Maryland, and share his knowledge with the extended Deering family that still lived around the area. He also promised him a job on one of the fishing boats that his family operated out of Annapolis. Excitedly, Jack accepted the offer, and the fifty-dollar bill that came along with it.

Captain Jack left Kinnakeet the next Saturday morning after a round of goodbyes with his A.A. family. He, and his single duffel bag, fit comfortably in the Theiss family Winnebago.

Twelve months later, Allen received a note from Jack. Enclosed with it was a Polaroid photo of Jack, standing proudly on the deck of a shiny new fishing trawler. In the note, Jack said that he was the captain of his own ship once again, and was celebrating 18 months of sobriety.

Allen showed the picture and letter around. There were many doubters.

But Laura White toasted the news with a smile, a piece of baklava, and a glass of water. Two days later she mailed a box containing a congratulatory note, and a dozen pieces of baklava, to the return address on the envelope.

WKIN

Good evening listeners, and welcome to WKIN, radio Kinnakeet. This is your host, Will E., here to take you through this hurricane Delores night. Along with me is our usual daytime engineer, Beth, who is filling in for our usual nighttime engineer, Paul. He made the intelligent decision to evacuate the island this morning along with his wife and children. And quite frankly, I hope most of our usual late night listeners have also moved to safety inland. But we'll be with you during my usual 9:00 p.m. until 2:00 a.m. Friday night time slot, and if you can't sleep we hope we can keep you company and share some classic tunes.

It's going to be a rough night as I'm sure you all know. The National Weather Service now says this category three storm will hit us head-

on sometime in the next hour or so. It's already a real mess out there, and we'll try to keep you informed as the evening goes by and the storm pays a visit to our special little corner of paradise. In the meantime, try to relax, and stay safe while you listen to a specially selected evening playlist of classic rhythm and blues. We'll start off with a hit from Little Milton from 1965 to get you in the right mood. Here's - We're Gonna Make It.

Will punched the button on the computer to start the music, hit the mic off button, then opened the intercom mic to the engineer booth and looked to his right. Beth was smiling, standing at her workstation and looking at him from behind the glass window.

"And off we go. Thank you, Beth for being here. I was preparing to do the show by myself, but it's so nice to have your help." Will shook his head, long gray hair flopping around his collar. "Though I have to say, I question your judgment."

Beth's smile disappeared briefly, then returned a bit brighter. "Yeah, well, maybe I do too. We'll see in a few hours. But I thought I should be here, the new kid on the block and all. Kind of wanted to see what it was like to ride out a hurricane, this being my first. I've heard so much from people in the last few days, both ways."

"Well," Will said, "I'd bet about 95 percent of those people have hightailed it off the island.

Even a lot of those who told you about the thrill of riding out a storm.”

“But . . .” Beth tilted her head and put her finger to her lips. “you’re still here.”

Will nodded, his frown hidden for a moment as he looked toward the window ahead of him. “Yeah, and I question my judgment too. I just have this strange idea about the station being an important source of information for the community in a crisis, which this is certainly going to be.”

Beth lowered herself to her chair, but kept her focus on Will as he turned back in her direction. “Have you stayed on the island during a hurricane before?” she asked.

“I have,” Will said. “A couple of tropical storms and one hurricane that mostly petered out before it hit land here. I think it was only a category one when it hit. The bad one that did so much damage down in Hatteras and Frisco was well before I got here.”

“Was it scary being here during those?” Beth glanced toward the window of her office as she spoke, though she couldn’t see outside.

“Absolutely. I wasn’t working at the station then. Just stayed at home and watched and listened.” Will peeked at the countdown timer on the computer screen in front of him. He held his hand up in the general direction of Beth, and when the timer hit zero he hit “play” for a commercial before the next song on the list. He decided to change the topic to try to ease some of what he perceived as Beth’s understandable anxiety. "So, how long have you worked at the station?"

"About three months, now."

"I'm sorry we didn't get a chance to meet before this." Will said.

A moment later they both startled and looked toward the north side of the building as an object of some size crashed into the outside of the wall. "Might have just lost a piece of siding or two," Will said, his hands unconsciously gripping the table in front of him. So much for easing her anxiety. "So, like I said, I wish we could have met under better circumstances."

"That's okay," Beth said, her eyes still studying the north wall. "They were going to have some kind of welcoming gathering, but that got canceled when COVID flared up."

"Well, I've heard good things about you. And, again, I'm glad to have you here." Will took a quick look at the countdown. He had 85 seconds. He looked back at his visibly worried companion. "I'm going to go peek out the front door. Be right back." He slipped out of the broadcast studio and into the small reception area just inside the front door.

Prior to COVID, visitors, mostly school children, waited in this room for the chance to experience first-hand how the engineers and disc jockeys went about sending out the words and music on the magic radio airways. There were few visitors for his late night program. Just an occasional fan stop-by.

The building had served as a three-bedroom house for the first 72 years of its existence before the radio station moved in five years ago. The upstairs rooms were now offices for the administration and sales staff. It was on the ocean side of Route 12, two rows from the beach on a narrow stretch of land. It had been three rows back when it was built, but Mother Nature had removed a long row of ocean-front houses. The front door opened onto a small grass and weed filled sandy lawn, with Route 12 just beyond.

Will pushed the door open with considerable effort and almost lost the door, and his footing, as a gust of wind yanked it and him toward the porch. He quickly regained control, and after just a brief look into the darkness, broken only by the few lights from the gift shop and bookstore across the street, and the flash of some unknown object, perhaps a flying trashcan, sailing cattycorner across the road through the rain, he tugged the door and retreated back into the safety inside. He brushed a hand through his hair and regained his composure before walking back into the studio.

"It's really blowing out there," he said, glancing toward Beth, whose expression conveyed her concern. "Not a night to be out and about." He knew as he said it that he had just made the understatement of the year. Beth nodded her agreement as he reclaimed his seat.

He watched the timer count down, then pushed the mic button.

This is Will E. back with you, along with Beth our engineer. We hope you're staying safe and indoors this evening. But we invite you to give us a call if you see something or hear something that we might pass along to our listeners. If the power goes out in your area, or you see some major damage or hazard like a road blockage, feel free to give us a call and we'll let everyone know. Deputy Carl Hopkins is out there keeping an eye on things and we expect a call from him before too long to fill us in on road conditions and other safety issues. But we know at least part of what he's going to say - stay home and away from windows.

Now, let's move along to a little song from Dee Clark from 1961. He was out in a driving rainstorm one evening and composed his classic, Raindrops, *to the rhythm of the windshield wipers on his car. I think you'll like it. Enjoy.*

Will pushed the keys on the keyboard and turned back to Beth. "So, tell me, how'd you end up here in beautiful Kinnakeet?"

Beth shot him an ironic smile and shook her head. She sat down and rubbed her forehead, pushing a few strands of brown hair out of her eyes. "It's a long story. You don't need to hear it all, but the short version is . . . well, I'm afraid it's fairly typical. A college love affair gone bad. Very bad. My boyfriend became increasingly possessive after graduation. I took a job where he wanted to be, even though it wasn't a good job for me. I tried to make things work, but eventually I had to get a restraining order to keep him away from me."

"And how did that work out?"

"Not so great. But the second time they arrested him they put him in jail long enough for me to move here. I'd been looking for jobs and had come here to interview, but unfortunately he found out that I'd been here for the interview. He made the usual threats, but when he went to jail I got some friends to help me pack up and move." Beth turned her head and made a quick wipe of her eyes. Will noticed but decided not to go there.

"Where were you living then?" he asked.

"I was in Cleveland."

Will debated for a moment, then decided to ask. "Any signs of him since you moved here?"

"I . . . don't think so. I did see a car drive by my house one day that looked a lot like his, but I only got a quick look at it out the window. That was about a week ago, so . . . I'm not going to worry about it." Her eyes told a different story, and after a couple seconds she continued. "But I live in an older residential neighborhood, so a strange car driving by is somewhat unusual."

Will immediately understood why she was primed to be suspicious, but it was probably healthy to be that way. Time to change the tone. "Where do you live?"

"Over by the Methodist Church. Near the harbor." A bit of color seemed to be trying to come back into her cheeks.

"Interesting. I live near there too. What street?"

"Soundview." Her voice perked up a bit.

"I live two streets over, on Turtle Drive."

"That's a much nicer street. The house I live in is a bit run down. But you probably know how hard it is to find a year-round rental here in Kinnakeet, or anywhere close. I was lucky to find this one. The old 'beggars can't be choosers thing'."

"You're right. Hopefully it's okay for a while."

"Oh, it is. Fortunately no creepy-crawlies or slithering house guests keeping me awake at night. Yet." A quick smile.

Will had dealt with a lot of people in his 61 years on this planet, but Beth had one of the most expressive faces he'd ever seen. Maybe some people wear their hearts on their sleeves, Beth wore her's on her face.

"Coming out in five," Beth said, alerting him to the end of the song. Will nodded and opened his mic.

Time to pick up the pace a little bit. This next song was co-written by Marvin Gaye and you can hear him tickling the ivories on the recording. This is something hopefully we can all do a little bit tomorrow morning – from 1964, here's Dancing in the Street *by Martha and the Vandellas.*

"So, how did you come to live in Kinnakeet?" Beth asked after the music began. "I already know you're not a native."

Will rocked back in his chair and closed his eyes for a moment. He considered how to keep the story short. And, if not sweet, at least not too sour. When he opened his eyes he grabbed the pen on the table in front of him and started doodling on the yellow pad that he pulled from the drawer. Finally, he made eye contact with Beth for just a moment. Then back to the doodling.

"I was a minister, in the Army. Served 31 years. Lutheran. First years were pretty interesting. A little travel around the world, a lot of time stateside. Then Iraq. Sent there just as everything started happening. On the front lines. Not too bad there. It was over pretty quickly. Then Afghanistan. Again, on the front lines with the troops. Spent a lot of time with a lot of very scared boys. They came over there poorly prepared and felt like sitting ducks for IEDs and snipers. And they were. The units I was with saw a lot of causalities. Young boys, 19, 20 years old, saw their friends blown to pieces, or losing arms, or legs. I was supposed to help them make sense of it, and see it all as part of God's grand plan."

Will paused and looked at the scribbles on the pad. Not much different than the ones he drew five years ago.

"Got fairly close to a handful of boys a few years ago who were from Minnesota. Grew up

Lutheran. Found out I was and came to talk to me several times when they first got there. Both individually and as a group. They were scared, but had enough macho in them that they figured they were there to kick ass, then go home and go to college or trade school on their army benefits. Then . . . one by one, we started losing them. First one dead to a sniper, second one shot in the neck and arm, but survived, barely. Third one blown up when a woman walked up to where he and two other guys were on guard duty and blew them all up." Will paused for a breath, then rocked back in his chair. "The others were coming to me for comfort and explanations. I was supposed to help them. They felt like sacrificial lambs. I did the best I could, but . . ."

Will looked at the timer. Still 29 seconds. He looked back at his scribbles. He didn't want to look at Beth.

"Then, one day, two more of them. Their truck was hit by a mortar shell. One had massive injuries, but lived. The other one lived for a couple hours, but died before they could ship him out. I was holding his hand when he died." Again, Will looked at the scribbles. Ugly.

"So, I decided that was it. I just couldn't do it anymore. I told my C.O. that I needed to get out. They needed to replace me with someone younger with a little stronger faith. Fortunately, he understood, and a week later I was stateside. They tried to keep me in. Assigned me to help train other ministers and priests headed over there. But they quickly realized I couldn't do that. So, three months of waiting, and I was out. My wife had the house picked out here and under contract when I came home. We moved here five years ago."

"That's fascinating," Beth said. "You really went through a lot." This time her voice conveyed as much concern as her face. She seemed not to know what else to say for a moment, then perked up. "And how long have you worked for the station?"

"Just under a year. Started off doing Friday night jazz, then the show transformed into R&B as it seemed the late night audience was more into that."

Will looked at the screen, punched the buttons, and waved to Beth. *Welcome back. I hope you're safe, warm, and maybe cuddling up close to someone to help get you through the night. I imagine some of you might be drifting off to sleep with the radio on to keep you company. I hope and pray you can sleep through this storm. Remember, we'll get through this together. Let's continue with a song that singer Eddie Floyd and his guitarist Steve Cropper put the finishing touches on while staying at the Lorraine Motel in Memphis, Tennessee. From 1966, let's* Knock on Wood.

A mere 50-yards to the south of the station, Heather Michaels, D.V.M. smiled, and literally knocked on the wooden railing of the steps

leading down from her apartment to the hospital section of the Shoreline Pet Clinic and Hospital. She'd found over the two years that she'd been in practice in Kinnakeet that the animals in the cages seemed comforted by the sound of music and kept the radio on 24/7 to one of the island stations. Her nighttime favorite was WKIN because of the different music they played each night of the week. Friday night was probably her favorite. She'd met Will on a number of occasions and found him to be a likeable and gentle soul. His chocolate lab was a real sweetie.

This night she had three dogs and two cats in her care, in addition to her golden retriever, Molly. This was fewer than usual for the hospital, especially since COVID hit the island, but so many people had left over the last few days and taken their pets with them.

She knew that her patients could hear, better than she could, the frightening sounds of the storm, and that this would be a difficult night for them. She kept the overhead lights off, and navigated by flashlight, while she visited with each animal, offering some comforting words and a few moments of petting. The three that were able to eat each got a treat. Before leaving the room, she glanced at the reassuring green light on the emergency generator in the corner.

"So, did your wife leave the island?" Beth asked as she began attacking the glass that separated her and Will with a bottle of spray window cleaner and a fist full of paper towels.

"Yes. She and our dog left yesterday morning. She's staying at her sister's in Raleigh."

Line one lit up on the telephone, interrupting Beth's cleaning. She answered it, talked briefly, then turned back to Will. "It's Deputy Hopkins, for you."

"Got it," Will said, then punched the button on his phone. "Hey, Carl. What's happening?" He listened for a full minute, then said, "Got ya. I'll get the word out." He listened again, then said, "Thanks a lot. And you be safe out there. Take your own advice." As he hung up he looked at the monitor for a second then switched on his mic as he turned to look at Beth.

Welcome back you brave souls out there in Kinnakeet and wherever else on the island you may be picking us up. We just heard from Deputy Carl Hopkins. He said it's terrible out there. He's been holed up in the station for the last half-hour as the roads are impossible and impassable. The traffic lights are out, as is the electricity in maybe 20 percent of the area. Bigger power outages are coming soon. Anything that isn't tied down or nailed down is flying around and the sand blast off the beach is removing paint from almost everything. To no one's surprise, Route 12 is blocked with washover just north of the village and just south before Buxton. He advises everyone to stay inside, away from windows, and keep your emergency supplies and loved ones close. He's going to stay at the station, but there's nothing he, or any other emergency services workers, can do until this storm clears, which we hope will be in the next very few hours.

Beth and I are going to stay here with you. We have an emergency power generator at the station, so if the power goes out here, we should be off the air for only a few seconds, maybe a minute or so, until the generator kicks in. Hopefully your electricity stays on, or you've got a battery powered radio, and we can keep you company through the worst of this. So, buckle down, and lets listen to a few more R&B classics. Next up, Please, Please, Please, *by James Brown and the Famous Flames.*

For the next 16 minutes, Will and Beth talked about the station, the on-air and behind the scenes personnel, and the local merchants who bought advertising time. Will filled Beth in on what he knew about the history of the station and the other one on the island broadcasting from Buxton.

They listened to the howling wind through the walls of their supposedly soundproof studios, and mutually startled each time a UFO hit the outside of the building. They'd each made an effort, up to that point, to not talk about the storm and the building anxiety they felt. However, Will could see the apprehension on Beth's face. And, even over the intercom, Beth could hear the slight tremble in Will's voice. They both felt the building shake as they came out of the music.

Thank you for being with us out there in radio land. That last song, as I'm sure all you faithful listeners know, was Fonetella Bass with her 1965 number one hit, Rescue Me. *As you stay safe and warm indoors, lets continue with a great one from 1959, Brook Benton with,* It's Just A Matter Of Time.

As Will hit the play button, a quarter-mile north, Randy Grissom struggled, but finally got the door to his 2019 Range Rover closed. Fifteen minutes earlier, he'd made the belated decision to leave the island and his oceanfront home. He'd argued 36 hours ago about this issue with Rose, his wife of 51 years. As she packed to leave, he stated, accurately, that they'd stayed through numerous storms in their 11 years living in their retirement dream home. He added, inaccurately, that this one wasn't going to be any worse than several of those.

After Rose left, he sat on the deck overlooking the ocean, drinking and feeling righteous and abandoned, then slept like a baby. Today, he'd eaten a little lunch and drank his dinner. Once he made the decision to leave, he packed a small bag with underwear and a change of clothes, then packed a second bag with bottles of his favorite bourbons, all three of them.

He managed with considerable wind assistance, to get from his driveway to Highway 12 and turned north. Within 100-yards he was blown off the left side of the road into a drainage ditch that had eight inches of water in it. He had the sense to switch to four-wheel-drive and got back on the road. He was in the ditch again 30-yards later. He got out again, but the irrationality of his plan to drive the many miles to get off the island began to dawn on him. He spotted the strip mall just ahead at the corner and managed make the turn into the parking lot. He maneuvered behind the tee-shirt and souvenir store, and nestled the vehicle a foot away from the back of the brick building for protection from the wind.

He was found there, dead, the next morning. His blood alcohol level was 0.46. Whether his death should be counted as storm related was debated for several weeks.

"Beth, did you walk or drive to the station this evening?" Will was standing by the window in his studio staring out into the darkness through the one inch gap between the plywood boards that protected the window. He could feel the cold wind even through the plywood and glass.

"I walked. But it was a real experience. Why?"

"Just wondering. I walked too." He stepped away from the window and sat in his chair, then propped his feet up on the desk, consciously trying to look relaxed. "You know, each storm that we have changes the coastline. The sandbars change, the beaches on the ocean side get narrower, and, often houses and businesses on the sound side flood, even if they don't on this side. That circular motion of the hurricane whips the water up over in the sound and even a few inches of rainfall over there can make a big difference. It's usually the wind and the sand that does the damage on this side of the road, and the water that causes most of the problems on the other side."

Beth studied him for a moment. She was trying to read his mind. "Do you think the houses over where we live will be safe?"

After just a second, Will answered. "Yeah. I think ours will be. But those that are right up by the harbor, and the ones in the marsh area that aren't elevated could be in trouble."

"Sounds like it's going to be a real mess around here for the next few days."

"The next few months," Will said under his breath as he nodded. He touched the button for his on-air mic.

Welcome back. We haven't heard anything new from our listeners to report on the storm. The National Weather Service now says that the eye of the storm is minutes away from us. And from the look and sound of things outside I can believe it. We may have a few minutes of relative calm when we're in the center of the eye, but then the winds are likely to get even worse. So, please, stay safe and let's get through this. We'll start off this next piece of the playlist with Our Day Will Come *by Ruby and the Romantics, from 1963.*

As Will stood up to stretch his legs, the windows rattled and the building shook. Hard. He took his cell phone out of his pocket and stared at it. It didn't surprise him that there was no signal. He waved it at Beth and said, "No signal. Cell tower is either down or out of commission. That's why we haven't gotten any calls since . . ." Before he could finish the sentence the overhead florescent lights flickered for a couple seconds, then the building went dark. He stood frozen, looking in Beth's direction. Waiting.

Heather Michaels felt the clinic building shake too. Her power went out for a few seconds, but then the generator kicked in and the light beside her bed flickered back on, as did the small lights on the electronics in her room. But the radio stayed silent. She waited with anticipation, but after five minutes still nothing. She adjusted the dial slightly, and got static, telling her the radio still worked. She got her headphones out of the bottom drawer of the dresser and put them on. At least if she couldn't have the radio, she could try to block out the noise of the storm, and maybe even get some sleep.

It was a fitful night, but when Heather awoke at 5:50 a.m., Molly was making her 'I need to go outside' noise. She pulled on a pair of sweatpants and shirt, then headed downstairs to the clinic area, with Molly in close pursuit. She would make a quick trip out to the front yard, then get back inside and to the hospital for morning rounds, which involved dispensing medications and food, along with a little petting, and checking on wounds and surgical sites.

When she got to the front room she pulled on the boots she kept by the door, then the rain jacket she had stationed there. After putting the long leash on Molly, she opened the door and stepped outside. She immediately froze in her tracks. Even in the earliest morning light, the scene in front of her looked like war zone footage from a movie.

There was lumber, rocks, aluminum siding, sections of roofing, and tons of sand in the road and stacked up against the buildings across the street. Water, as much as a foot deep, was in every low-lying depression and hole. As she looked to her left, she saw the first house, just across and down the street, was missing its front porch and part of the roof. When she turned to her right, she immediately saw the building that housed the WKIN radio station was gone.

She let Molly do her thing in the light rain, then got her back in the clinic and unfastened the leash. She dashed back out the door and headed up Route 12, splashing through the water and stepping over countless pieces of debris of all shapes and sizes. She knew it would likely be days before the road was clear for traffic.

As she got near the front of what was left of the WKIN building, she saw a young woman wearing a raincoat, standing at the edge of the road with her arms wrapped tightly around herself, staring toward the remains of the building. A moment later she saw a man, stepping carefully through the rubble, pushing aside boards, pieces of plywood, and furniture. She rushed up to the woman and asked if she was okay. She got a meek, "Yes," but her body language, and especially her face, said otherwise.

Heather introduced herself and added that she lived just down the road, nodding toward the clinic. The woman slowly turned toward her and mumbled, "I'm Beth. I . . . I used to work here."

"Oh," Heather said, moving closer and reaching out to put her hand on Beth's shoulder, "I was listening to the station last night when the power went out and you went off the air." She turned toward the man, now standing frozen, looking down toward his feet and the refuse scattered around him. "Is that Will?" She got a slow nod in return.

"I'm so glad you got out of there before that happened," Heather said, watching Beth's eyes glisten with tears in the gray light.

"We . . . almost didn't." Beth wiped her eyes with her wet hand. "Will . . . he practically dragged me out of there. I didn't want to leave. I wanted to stay and see if . . ." her voice cracked for a moment, "the generator would kick on."

"Oh my God! You're so lucky you got out." Heather said, her own voice now a near whisper.

Beth nodded slowly. "We . . . we were just down the street when a blast of wind blew us into the wall of the hardware store. Will had just picked me up when we heard the building go down." Beth turned back to look at the building ruins laying in front of her. "We just stood there, leaning against the wall, and watched it all blow away." She turned her back to the debris and wiped her face with her arm.

"Oh, my!" Heather stepped back in shock and shot a quick glance at Will, then turned back to Beth. "Where did you go? How did you get there?"

"We managed to get to my house." Beth stammered, almost inaudibly. Then she took a breath and turned back to face Heather and the remains of the building. "Will said the gust that blew the building down might be the last one before the eye of the storm passed over us. It let up enough that we could get to my house . . . Hanging on to each other."

As they spoke, Will began making his way out of the wreckage. As he reached them, he acknowledged Heather with a slight nod, then handed Beth a metallic object he carried with him. She took it in her shivering hand, then held it up to examine it. "That's about all I could find," Will said.

It was a badly bent and scratched, engraved brass plate, given to Beth by the station manager on her first day of work. It read,

Beth Wyatt - Engineer
WKIN Radio

Beth's face collapsed and her eyes filled with tears. Will moved in to give her a hug.

COVID be damned, Heather thought, as she stepped into the pair and threw her arms around them.

The Fisherman

The first tug on the line yanked him out of his deliberations about the mess he'd left behind 45 minutes ago. Michael lifted the rod, set the hook, and felt the panic of the fish. The second, much bigger pull 10 seconds later, nearly tore the rod out of his hands. The fight was on.

He knew instantly this was a big fish. Hopefully a red drum, but maybe a shark. The initial bite felt like a little guy. His brain told him maybe a much bigger fish had attacked the smaller one struggling on the end of his line. Maybe the hook had slipped out of the first mouth and attached itself to a new lip. Or maybe the hook was now buried in the digestive tract of the big guy.

Fortunately, Michael remembered to adjust the drag on his reel almost immediately.

He needed to allow the fish some freedom to fight, lest he break the 20-pound test line, but not enough to strip the 400 yards of monofilament on the reel. A strong pull in the right direction by a fish even smaller than this would snap the knot between line and hook. Not enough play and the hook could also straighten allowing the fish to escape. His gear was set up for the keeper size drums he was hoping to catch.

"Come on, big guy! You know I've got you now," he shouted to the morning darkness as the line ripped off his reel. "Let's see who's the more intelligent being." However, he already suspected that luck, rather than intelligence, was likely to be the deciding factor in this battle. Especially if he was the winner.

The previous two days he, Paul, and Carlos had fished together. The first day from the pier, then yesterday at the Point. They'd caught their share. Michael maybe a few less than his companions. This morning the other guys were, hopefully, still cuddled up with their wives in the rental house. He and Pam had gotten into it at bedtime. After a sleepless night he'd decided he might as well head out early, even before the first light. The crew had talked about possibly fishing this morning at the first ramp north of Kinnakeet, but no firm decision had been made. He'd left no notice of where he was going, but hoped the guys would find him. And soon.

The steady pull and frequent jerks inflicting a parabolic bend in his rod confirmed this was a very big fish who was not happy. Michael wasn't happy either. He didn't have time.

His mind was trying to review everything he'd ever read or heard about fighting a big fish. In the four years he'd been surf fishing his biggest catch was a 37-inch shark. The 10-minute battle ended in disappointment that the defeated was a hammerhead shark and not a drum or flounder. The throbbing already registering from his shoulder told him this was a much larger opponent.

The fish swam north. Michael followed, splashing through the edge of the surf. His boots smacking the wet sand made a sound like a misfiring jalopy. He remembered to keep the rod level with the horizon and the butt pointing slightly south. However, the tip of the rod was following the fish.

When the fish stopped after maybe 200 yards, Michael was able to catch his breath. After a series of hard jerks the pulling stopped. The line went slack. Afraid he'd lost the fish, Michael raised the rod. To his relief, he felt resistance instead of the line slithering back in his direction.

The fish now seemed to be resting. Something he'd never heard about a fish doing. Or maybe he was thinking. Michael kept a steady pressure on the creature, but decided a rest period was not a bad thing. He could feel the hammering deep in his chest. An anxious five minutes passed.

"You are a smart one, old guy," he said to the fish as he walked toward him, taking up line.

"Why is it a guy?" his wife would ask if she was here. "Just because the fish is strong and wise enough to live a long time in a hostile environment doesn't mean it's a male." She would give this as another example of his unconscious, and sometimes conscious, sexism. And she would be right. Just as she was last night. He needed to do better.

The fish shook its head. The tip of the rod vibrated. A moment later the fish, who he now decided was a wise old girl, headed south. He raised the rod tip to the sky and reeled furiously to keep slack out of the line. As the fish passed him, hell-bent for the warmer waters of South Carolina, Michael nodded and declared, "I've still got you, old girl." He pointed the rod to the north and let the fish again take line. The reel screamed in protest. The lights of the pier were still visible, though the sky at the horizon had just begun to turn softly pink.

Michael took off running again. This time in the firm sand just above the edge of the waves. Twenty yards past where he'd dropped his bucket of bait, knife, and tackle box, the chase ended.

Now the fish seemed to be swimming in circles. Lazily trying to wrap the line around her tail and dislodge the hook. Or maybe there was something under the water to wrap around. An old plank from a shipwreck. Or a long lost cooler from a sport fishing boat.

For a moment Michael froze. His boots dug into the sand. He wanted this fish. But if the fish wrapped the line there would be nothing he could do. He'd be left with nothing but the classic fish story of the one that got away – after a 20-minute battle and a couple of sprints in the sand. If anyone asked how big the fish was he'd say he couldn't even guess, and leave it at that.

The story Paul and Carlos told him two nights ago about the state and world record red drum caught by a surf fisherman just north of the Kinnakeet pier flashed in his head. The story was validated by pictures and newspaper accounts retrieved online. The 94-pound monster was nearly the length of the lucky fisherman.

Michael had no illusions that his fish, as strong and mighty as it was, would challenge that record. And it wasn't even his fish yet. It was still its own master. At this point the hook was an inconvenience. A problem to be solved. One it had probably solved many times before. It was unrealistic to think a fish this size had never been hooked before.

"This time it's going to be different," he announced to the seagull who had abandoned its companions and wandered over, now 15 feet away, to observe and monitor the intruder. "She may be more experienced at this than I am, but I'm the human and she's just a fish." He wasn't sure, but thought perhaps the shrill *kuk-kuk-kuk* that the gull screamed back was mocking him. He realized the others who had hooked her were also humans.

Still on the hook, now apparently rested, the fish took off for the horizon. Michael raised the rod straight to the sky and kept tension on the line. His shoulder, and now his wrist, protested. Again, the fish tore dozens of yards of line from the reel. Long minutes passed as she zig-zagged her way toward the distant gulf stream.

He wondered now about the integrity of the knot he'd tied yesterday afternoon between line and hook.

Joining these two parties together needed to be done with care and patience. They each had to do their part. Weakness in any of the three – the line, the hook, or the knot marrying the two together, would cause the union to fail. It had happened to him before. He said a quick prayer that the knot would hold, then pulled the rod back toward him to slow down the fish. She showed no signs of tiring for another few minutes, but eventually turned.

This time, after a couple minute's rest, she swam directly back at him. He knew instantly this was her smartest move. It would be difficult, if not impossible, for him to reel fast enough to keep tension on the line. The hook would be loose and at risk of falling free. Especially if there had been some tearing of the tissue around where the hook was embedded, enlarging the hole.

His left hand spun the handle around the reel at warp speed. Still, the line hung loose off the end of the rod. She was winning. Or at least making her point. She was a very smart ol' gal.

It seemed she must be getting close to him. Then . . . there she was! A flash just beneath the peak of a wave not more than 20 feet in front of him. She filled the whole height of the wave. And several feet of its length. Then . . . she was gone in a heartbeat.

He knew he'd lost her, but continued to reel in line. It took almost a minute, but he felt tension again, followed by a strong pull. She was still there! Now headed south again.

He hadn't seen enough of her to be sure, but he thought she was a red drum. A huge one. Didn't see the classic dot in the area of the tail. He saw more of her front half than her back. But they'd made eye contact, and that shook him.

She didn't look angry or scared, as he would have expected. Rather more . . . questioning. It was as if her eye was asking his eye, "Why?"

He didn't like the question.

Twenty-five minutes ago he could have answered the question with confidence and assurance.

He was the human. She was a fish. Her existence was only to serve mankind as food.

Though he personally didn't eat fish, the other five people with him did. And that was okay.

But also, he was a man. Men were hunters. It was their job to kill the food and bring it in. And if the prey offered a challenge, the bigger the better! A defining feature of manhood, and status in the community, was determined by how he defeated, how he overcame, the challenges, then killed and brought home the food. It had been that way since men first walked the earth.

He had wanted to bring this giant fish home. To let Pam see this part of manhood. His manhood. A piece of the genetic XY programming.

He wanted Paul and Carlos to see him with the fish. Preferably see him land the fish. He'd wished at various points in the struggle that they were here. To see how he was handling the rod and meeting the challenges thrown at him. They would be cheering him on. And offering valuable advice.

But now, it was different. She was no longer food.

That moment of eye contact had made her . . . he struggled to define it. Not a fish. Not prey . . . but . . . another living thing. A very old one. One who'd met and survived countless challenges of her own that he could never fathom or understand. And now, in her old age, maybe she'd lost her edge. Lost whatever it was – speed, strength, agility – that had allowed her to survive this long. To defeat other, more skilled, fisherman who'd hooked her. To evade the predatory beasts of the ocean.

She deserved . . . respect. That was the only word that came to mind. Then . . . something inside him, something foreign, maybe somewhere in a part of his being he wasn't used to listening to, shouted out – *She deserves to live!*

If he could have, Michael would have taken a couple minutes to sit in the sand and think about that. But the run the fish was making demanded his full attention. A glance at his screaming reel showed maybe only 50 yards of line left. Out of 400.

While letting her take the remaining line would cause the knot at his reel to break, thus freeing her from him, it would leave her with the hook in her, perhaps in her gut, and 400 yards of line trailing behind her wherever she went. Eventually that line would tangle on something and she would be trapped. That was not a good ending – for him or the fish.

His only choice at this point was to run toward the fish, and at the same time tighten the drag and point the rod farther north. Apply more pressure. Push the strength of the 10-foot rod to its maximum. See if he could make it too hard for her to keep swimming away from him. Of course the rod could break and that would end the battle. The sound of a shattering rod was like a firecracker going off just a foot out of your hand. He'd heard it once before.

He did what he had to do. A 30-yard splashy sprint. The fish slowed. Then stopped.

Time for another rest period, maybe a minute or two. A quarter of the sun was peeking over the horizon and the sky over the ocean was now in bloom. He could see the beach now all the way to the first house to the south, then the pier in the distance. He tucked the rod under his arm and put his hands on his knees. Immediately the fish headed back at him.

He grabbed the rod and reeled furiously. He fought through the spasm in his wrist and the cramping in his fingers. But he couldn't keep up with the slack.

The fish didn't come for a visit this time. When Michael got all the slack on the reel she was probably 150 yards to the north. After another couple minutes, she stopped and swam in circles for a while. Trying that tactic again. This gave Michael breathing, and thinking, time.

It took him only a minute to come to the conclusion that this battle had to end soon. For the fish's sake as well as his. Somehow, the idea that the fish deserved to live had settled in and taken possession of him.

Perhaps if he gave a hard yank on the line the hook would rip out of the fish's lip. *If* it was in her lip. That wound would heal.

But what if the hook was in her gut? What if she had swallowed a smaller fish that had struck the bait, as he suspected, and the hook was now somewhere deeper inside her? That the hook was still lodged in her, despite her multiple and educated attempts to dislodge it, suggested this was likely. The hook might not release and could cause a grave injury. Or it would release and tear her insides as he pulled it away. Perhaps bringing part of her guts with it.

"No, I can't do that," Michael proclaimed, staring at his line disappearing into the waves.

He had to bring this fish, this monster fish, this living creature, and worthy opponent, to hand. His pliers were in his back pocket. He would do whatever he could to free the hook and release her with minimal harm.

She had to be tired. He was. His right arm, shoulder, and wrist throbbed. His left hand was nearing the point of uselessness from all the frantic spinning of the reel handle. He had no way to understand how her body felt.

Conventional fishing wisdom was that the shorter the fight, and quicker the release, the better chance the fish had to survive. Michael didn't know how long they had been linked together, but it had to be more than an hour.

He wondered how long it had taken that man to land the 94-pound red drum. That hadn't been mentioned in the articles, or he'd missed it. That fish had been dragged ashore, hauled into Kinnakeet, and hung up by its jaw for weighing and pictures. That was not going to happen to this lady.

A plan fell into place as they both rested. He would tighten the drag and apply as much pressure as he could to bring her in. He would push the rod close to its limit and use as much strength as he could muster to reclaim line onto his reel and resist the fish's fight. If the knot failed that would be fine. She'd have only the hook left inside her. She would survive that.

Perhaps it would help if he explained this to her. He shouted in her direction.

"Hey, beautiful old lady. We've got to bring this to an end. I'm going to release you. Please, let go of your instinct to fight and work with me."

He doubted if that helped any. But it made him feel better.

For another several minutes the fish went through her repertoire of tactics. But each one was a little weaker, or shorter. Michael had two short runs, up, then down the beach. But he was gaining line on the reel.

Then, after one last jerk she seemed to give up, and drifted in his direction.

"Oh no! I hope I haven't killed you," he screamed at her. "Please don't die!" He wondered if fish had heart attacks.

A moment later she appeared at the surface of the water – her tail popped through the crown of a wave first, then the top of her head. Maybe 20 yards away. The next wave pushed her toward him. He waded out knee deep in the water and grabbed the line hanging loose off the end of his rod and pulled. She drifted toward him. A swish of her tail brought her still closer.

"Work with me baby," he said. She was now five feet away. He pulled the line again and her mammoth body slid just in front of him. He could see the monofilament disappear into her mouth, but couldn't see the hook. They made eye contact again.

This time what he saw was surrender. And that both pleased and, at the same time, angered him.

She was doing what he'd asked her to do. She was coming to him to let him find the hook, remove it, and let her go free.

Yet, this grand old lady of the sea, this valiant, intelligent, matriarch, who had lived so many years, and produced countless offspring, should never have to surrender. Certainly not to a mediocre fisherman and human such as himself. He did not deserve her surrender.

She'd given him the gift of an experience of a lifetime. An opportunity to test himself. To test what he'd learned about catching a fish. To test his stature as a hunter. As a man. He would never forget a single moment of their battle. One of the best experiences of his life.

But now, with her surrender, she was giving him the opportunity to measure his life, his value as a human being, on a different scale. The scale of the meaning of life. To be measured on that scale must have something to do with compassion and empathy. To be a living being in a world of other, no less valuable, living beings.

She should live as many more years as her genetic programming would allow. She'd proven her worth as one of God's most noble creatures simply by living as long as she had. She should be allowed to die a dignified and painless death burrowed in the soft, comforting sand of the ocean floor. He knew the least he could do was allow her that opportunity. Then nature would take its course.

He pulled the line and she glided up next to him. He grabbed the line with his left hand and followed it into her open mouth. Almost a foot inside he felt the hook. It was buried in what must have been her jaw, not her lip. He dropped the rod and grabbed his pliers. Now he followed the line with his right hand and grabbed the hook with the tip of the pliers. He worked it back and forth, as gently as he could, until it slid free. She was drifting downward, almost motionless. The waves had little effect on her. He pulled his hand out and dropped the pliers. That was only the first part of his task.

As quickly as he could, he bent over and reached beneath her massive belly with first one hand, then the other, and cradled her. His open hands were four feet apart. He knew his job now was to move her back and forth to force water, with its life-giving oxygen, into her gills and ultimately her blood vessels. She needed both the oxygen and some recovery time to let her muscles regain sufficient strength to swim again.

Holding her like this he began to cry.

"Come on, old lady. You can do it," he whispered through the tears in the direction of her head. After a minute he felt her body shift. Then, another minute later, she twisted so that her head, and eye, were closer to his.

This time the eye-to-eye contact was brief. Only a second. But the message he got spoke volumes to his soul.

A few seconds later her great tail swished and she swam slowly out of his arms. Michael stepped aside as the giant fish, now finally *his* fish as he let it go, headed out to the ocean depths.

As he gathered his rod and pliers, then walked back to the shore, Michael wondered what he would tell his fishing buddies, and Pam, about the fish. And about the most meaningful hour and a half of his life.

Bathed in the warm glow of a new Kinnakeet morning, he decided he'd tell them nothing. The story, the experience, and the lessons learned, were no one's business. They would remain forever between him and his mighty fish.

Escape

Greg met her in the driveway as she stepped out of the Lexus. She looked every bit as beautiful as the hundreds of pictures he'd seen of her over the last few years. Even casually dressed, in pink jeans and a sea-green linen pullover, she was stunning. The hug was a bit awkward.

"It's so nice to see you, Allie," he said. "It's been a while."

"And it's so nice to see you again, after all these years!" she replied, that so familiar smile lighting up everything around her. "I'm so glad you returned my call and let me come for a visit."

"Of course. Wouldn't miss seeing you for the world. We've got a lot of catching up to do." He stepped to the rear of the car as the trunk popped open, and removed the suitcase that she pointed out.

She nodded and whispered "Thank you," then stepped aside and said, "The last time we were together was . . ."

"The summer after our sophomore year in college." Greg had revisited much of their time together since her call two days ago.

"That's right. You remembered." She grinned, then added, "I told you I wasn't going back to school so I could pursue a career in music."

"And how'd that turn out?" he said with a soft snicker. They both laughed as he closed the trunk and motioned her to the stairway to the house, then fell in behind her.

In the ensuing 13 years since their last time together, she'd recorded eight number one selling albums, posted 19 number one hits on the pop and country charts, completed five tours (the last four international and lasting four months each), and won more Grammys, CMAs, American Music Awards, and songwriting awards than any female on planet earth. She also had an Oscar nomination. Her music had sold over 30 million albums in the U.S. alone, and over 150 million singles worldwide. She was known all over the world simply as, "Allie."

He gave her a quick tour of the first floor of the house, showing her the pool table and dart board in the game room, passed quickly by the laundry room, then the first guest bedroom. On the second floor, he dropped her bag in the master guest bedroom with the ocean view and sliding glass door to the deck. He briefly showed her the *en suite* bathroom with Jacuzzi tub and separate glass-walled shower, then let her peek in the other bedroom, his studio room, and the exercise room. Then he led her up the stairs into the large living room, with the striking all-glass wall, that looked out over a dune to the calm ocean just over a hundred yards away.

"This is incredible," she exclaimed. "This view is . . . to die for!" She rushed to the wall and stared out.

"It is pretty nice," he said, as he opened a sliding door and followed her out to the wooden deck. "I spend a lot of time out here. The house is really too big for one person, but it was the location here in Kinnakeet, and the view that sold me. The ocean has a real calming, and sometimes almost meditative, effect. And, as beautiful as it is during the day like this, the night is just incredible. You can see literally thousands of stars with the naked eye."

He stepped away from her, then turned to watch the sunlight and breeze play with her blond hair while she leaned on the railing. After a moment, she closed her eyes and took a deep breath.

"I love it," she said once her eyes opened again a half-minute later. "The rhythm of the waves, the sound of the birds, the salt in the air. It's just what I imagined it would be."

Greg thought it was a bit odd that she'd imagined the view from the deck of his house, but said nothing. Maybe she was just referring to the generic experience of the ocean.

He asked her to join him for a brief tour of the rest of the house; showed her his bedroom, the office, then the kitchen and dining area. He suggested she relax back on the deck for a minute while he fixed them a drink. She requested a diet soda and he prepared the same for himself. He happened to have the one that she was a spokesmodel for on hand. Three minutes later he was back on the deck, in the second wooden rocking chair by her side.

"Were you surprised when I sent you the private message on Facebook then called you?" she asked after accepting the drink. They both watched a seagull glide in front of a wave then land on the dune a few yards in front of them.

"I certainly was. But very happy you did. I can't think of anyone I'd rather have appear out of the blue."

She shifted slightly in the chair in his direction. "You called me Alison when we were on the phone. I liked that. It reminded me of . . . I guess our time together back then, and when life was a lot simpler."

"I'm sorry. I guess a part of my brain still thinks of you that way, and it just slipped out."

"No! Please! Don't apologize," she said. "In fact, I'd like it if you'd call me that when we're together. I'd like to just be Alison with you."

"Okay. I'll try to do that." He nodded slowly and sipped his drink. "You know . . . I've followed your career all these years. That's a pretty easy thing to do with all the media attention you get for practically everything you do."

"Yeah," she paused, and a slight frown marred the face with the perfect skin. "And I've followed you, though that's a lot harder. You don't post much on Facebook, and I haven't seen you on any other social media. But there have been a few newspaper articles about you. Mostly in the Wall Street Journal."

"Really? You've followed me?" He was surprised. They'd known each other since the age of nine, but their lives had drifted worlds apart since that last summer so many years ago.

"Yes. You've been in my mind more than you could imagine. You were my best friend all the way through school. You were the one guy, the one person, I could talk to. You were always there for me, whenever I needed someone to talk to, or a shoulder to cry on. You were my touchstone through all those teenage ups and downs. And then those two summers when we were home from college, you were still the person I wanted to be around, the person I wanted to talk to." She paused for a sip. "There's been many times since then I've needed that, and thought of you, and how kind you always were to me."

Greg was a bit flabbergasted. "I've thought about you a lot too. You were my best friend."

"You know," she said, turning to look at him instead of the ocean, "you could have been my first. My first lover. I was ready toward the end of our senior year, and during both of those summers."

It took Greg a moment to process that piece of information. He'd wondered, but . . . "You had boyfriends who were so much . . . and they were . . ." He didn't know quite how to put it. "And I was –"

"Too shy," she inserted.

"That," he agreed with a chuckle, "plus I'd say generally too immature." His thoughts drifted for just a moment to what might have been. "I valued you so much as a friend I didn't want to spoil it by trying to take the relationship there and get rejected. I didn't want you to think that's all I wanted from you."

"Well," she said with a grin, "none of those boyfriends treated me the way you did, and I was just smart enough to know I didn't want them that way." She reached over to grip his shoulder, then caught his eye and offered a slightly sad smile. "But that particular ship has long set sail." She squeezed then let go. "I'm actually here for you to be my touchstone again. You were always so good at listening and providing feedback to help me sort out my feelings, and that's mainly what I need now. If you're willing."

"I am," he said, without hesitation. It would be easy to step back into that role with Alison. "Go ahead. This is a wonderful setting for a talk."

She took a sip of her drink and stared out to the sea in front of her. "I feel like I'm at a crossroads in my life," she began. "I've been at my parents' house for a week, thinking things over. But it's been coming on for quite a while." She looked back to him for a moment. "They said to say hello, by the way."

He smiled and nodded. They were good folks. He'd spent many hours at their house and they'd been nothing but kind to him.

It was a minute or so before she started again. "I'm kind of burned out on the whole celebrity and performer thing. I'm tired of having every minute of my life taken up with the demands and expectations – the long tours, the rehearsals, the photoshoots, the video production, the interviews, all the millions of meetings with everybody. Flying from coast-to-coast for TV appearances. So many people depending on me, and so many commitments. It seems like every minute is taken, all day, every day when I'm not on tour. And it's just about the same then."

She paused for a breath. "I don't even know how many people work for me, probably dozens, maybe hundreds, if you count the production company. I have two, not one, but two," she illustrated this point with a pair of fingers, "full-time people who monitor and control the social media accounts, webpage, and fan club. They always want to show me what people are saying about me and get my input on what to post." She stopped to rock and think for a moment, then started up again. "My manager, my agent, the accountants, the financial advisors, the lawyers, all the product people who want me to endorse or model . . . It's gotten overwhelming." Her voice sounded fatigued.

Greg nodded and reached out to touch her arm. She leaned into his touch before he took the hand away. "It's not surprising you're overwhelmed. That's a lot. And you've been doing it for quite a few years."

"Yes, and I'm just tired of it. I can't go anywhere without a driver and at least one security person. You don't know how hard it was to get the team to let me come here by myself. It's like I have to ask permission to drive my own car to visit my parents, or you, by myself."

"They're all trying to look out for you, I guess."

"I know that. And I understand. But it's too much. At least this COVID thing has given me a little bit of a break. I spent most of the last year at my house in Los Angeles, and some in the New York apartment. But even then, I've been working. Zooming meetings almost every day, and doing a little writing. The band has been rehearsing on FaceTime together, and that's weird, but we've also gotten together some in Nashville to work on the next album. But . . ." She closed her eyes for a couple moments. "I've gotten back in touch, a little bit, with what it's like to have some personal time, some quiet time. And I've liked it."

Greg nodded. "So now you're thinking about . . .?"

Her reply was quick. "Quitting, retiring, walking away." She paused for a moment, then added, "and having a private life."

He feigned astonishment. "You mean without the paparazzi cameras in your face everywhere you go?"

"Yes, that would be wonderful. And without all the fans insisting on autographs and a selfie with me." She closed her eyes and shook her head for a second. "Don't get me wrong, the fans are all nice, at least most of them, but it's just so constant. I can't go out to dinner, or for a run, without people coming up to me, just to get a little something personal from Allie. Even when I wear a hat and big, dark sunglasses."

"You're too beautiful and recognizable to escape notice, at least most places." He watched for her reaction, got none, but then realized she'd probably been told she was beautiful by a million people, including at least a dozen fashion magazine editors and a thousand photographers. It didn't register with her anymore.

"So . . . you're ready to pull the plug, or still undecided?" he asked.

"I'm . . . still undecided. And that's why I'm here." She paused and turned her chair toward his. Their legs were almost touching. "You've done what I want to do. You've had the big career, put in the long hours, made all the money, and then you sold the company you started and walked away. Right?"

Greg studied her face for a moment. Before he could respond she added, "At least that's what I've gathered from what's out there about you. You're a pretty private person."

His brows puckered just a bit. "Maybe you could tell me what's 'out there' about me?"

"Really not much. You started your own cloud-based computer software development company about a year after you graduated with your master's degree. The programs you developed sold like crazy to medical practices, accounting firms, law firms, engineering companies, and other places like that. You grew the business, added associates who also developed very popular programs, sold the company to a couple of them for a few million, and walked away about a year ago. Then you moved here to the beach and have been living the good life."

A big grin swept across Greg's face. He thought that was a pretty good ten second summary of about ten years of his life. "That's . . . actually pretty close. I was very lucky. You know the saying, 'timing is everything?' Well, that seemed to be the case for me. I still have a small piece of the company and do a little consulting and training for them, but that doesn't take up much time. I have a lot of freedom to do what I want."

"And what do you do with that freedom?" Allie asked.

"I sit here and watch the ocean. I take long runs and walks on the beach. And, I enjoy painting. I paint on glass. I took a number of classes and workshops over the years, and now that I actually have time to do it, I really enjoy it. Once the COVID is over I'll be doing some travelling. Going the places I want to go and taking a lot of pictures of things that I might want to come back here and paint."

"See . . ." Allie's face lit up and she stroked his knee. "That sounds wonderful. I'd love to be doing something like that. The beach here is just amazing. I could live on the beach. And I've seen the couple of pictures you've posted on Facebook of your paintings. They're beautiful. You're really talented."

"Thank you," he said with his head shaking. "But my talent is minimal compared to yours."

"Different, not less," she said with a finger wag.

Greg thought that was probably her stock reply to that conversation. But it was a good one. "Okay. We can agree to disagree about that."

"Fine." She took a drink of her soda and studied the horizon. "One thing that isn't out there about you is anything about relationships.

I expected to get here and meet your wife or girlfriend."

"That's right. I've tried to keep that part of my life out of the media. Not that there's much of a story there." He took a moment to consider how much detail she needed to know. "I've been in a couple fairly long-term relationships. The last one ended just after I decided to retire. She had a pretty powerful career going, and decided she wanted to stay with it. She's in Chicago now."

Allie frowned slightly. "You haven't been seeing anyone since you moved here?"

"I've been on exactly two sort-of dates. Two different women. One dinner with each of them." He stood up and leaned against the railing. "You, on the other hand, seem to have had several boyfriends over the years."

"Yeah, hundreds, if you want to believe the tabloids." She got up and stood close beside him. "Every time there's a picture taken of me with a guy beside me, or even nearby, the headlines scream about Allie's new boyfriend. That's another thing I'm really tired of." She ran both hands through her hair, then gripped the railing. "I've had what I would consider three relationships that I thought had some potential. But, I learned you can't maintain a relationship while touring. And, when all your time and energy is devoted to your career, you only attract guys that want something from you that's not particularly healthy."

"I can imagine."

"Yeah. They either want my money and me to support them, or they want me or my people to promote their career or business. Or, they want what they think is the fame of being 'Allie's boyfriend.'"

"And none of that is good for you."

"Right." She looked skyward for a moment and sighed. "I want to be in a relationship, and be in love, but I've decided I don't want to be with anybody in the music or entertainment industry. They're all self-centered and . . . well, maybe I am too. Maybe you have to be, to some degree, in this business. But, I also don't want to be with anybody who needs me to support them. I want someone who can see me, and treat me, as an equal. And, I want to see them that way. And that's hard to find."

"It sure is." Greg readily understood that point. He'd been there. "Especially for someone in your position. You're probably the most famous woman in the world, with the possible exception of Michelle Obama, and certainly one of the richest."

Allie grew silent, started rocking, and seemed to concentrate on the sights and sounds in front of her for a full minute. The seagull was staring at them.

"Yes. But you know the fame is all an illusion, don't you? It can disappear in a heartbeat. The next five Allies are lined up and anxious to take my place. I can be replaced in the music world in no time. And that's okay with me! And, when you come right down to it, the money doesn't matter that much. Right now, I'd give 98 percent of it away for a private life with someone I love who loves me."

Greg was afraid to glance even slightly in her direction. "You sound like you're pretty close to making that retirement decision."

"I am. But, I want to hear about your experience. Are you glad you retired? Are there things you miss about working and having all that, I don't know . . . maybe recognition that you accomplished something meaningful? And having those people in the industry looking up to you? And all those employees depending on you?"

It took just a second for Greg to form his response. "Short version – yes, I'm glad I retired when I did. And, no, there's nothing I miss about the work. I still have my finger in the pie, and can do a little bit when, and if, I want to. But, I enjoy the freedom a whole lot more. That sense of power and influence you have when you build a business, and have articles written about you in the Wall Street Journal, is also an illusion. It's been really easy for me to let go of that and let it float away. But . . . that's me. It might be harder for you." Now he could look at her.

"Maybe so." Allie seemed to drift for a moment. Greg took advantage of the silence.

"Hey. It's getting a little cool out here. How about this? Let's move inside and take a break for a couple minutes. I was going to fix dinner for us, but I have another idea maybe you'd go for."

"Okay. What is it?" Allie turned and stepped inside when he slid the door open.

"I'd like to take you out to dinner at one of the local restaurants. Let's put that 'I can't go anywhere without being recognized and hassled' theory to the test. I think it might be a little different here in Kinnakeet than in New York or Las Angeles. At least during what they call the shoulder season, which is what we're in now. It'll be different in a couple months. It's mostly locals here now, and I think even if some of them recognized you they'd respect your privacy. I could be wrong, but if you're willing, we could have some great seafood."

Allie gave him the smile that had graced a thousand magazine covers. "Sure. I'm game."

Twenty minutes later they were seated in one of Greg's favorite restaurants, the Ocean Bistro. They'd been greeted by the hostess and led through the mostly occupied tables to a space near the back of the house without anyone seemingly recognizing the star in their presence. The masks they were wearing may have helped with that.

By mutual agreement, they limited their dinner discussion to reminisces about their earlier time together. They laughed about Allie's pain and agony at not getting the lead role in the junior-year musical production. Of course, she had the lead in the senior musical, *Annie Get Your Gun*, and several other productions of the music department. They joked about all the piano and guitar practice sessions Greg sat through to offer encouragement, starting when Allie was 11 years old. They also made fun of Greg's nerdy ways back then, and the crisis of his first, and only, high school grade of B; in a science class no less.

Allie talked about her two years as a student in the Musical Arts department at Penn State University. She told Greg about the local bands she sang and played with during those years, and the wonderful professor who gave her such strong support and encouragement. When she told the professor she would not return for her junior year, she connected her with a New York based song-writer she knew. She and Allie hit it off, and together, over the next five years, they wrote several of her hit songs. Allie kept in touch with the professor and visited with her whenever she was in town. She also accepted her invitation to speak to a class of students at each visit, and found time for a song or two at the end of their time together.

Greg offered little about his undergraduate and graduate school years, knowing it would be quite boring to anyone not into computers. However, what he did talk about Allie gave her rapt attention to, and asked intelligent questions. He also kept the story of the development of his company brief, preferring to listen to Allie and her stories.

They enjoyed a delightful dinner – blackened tuna for Allie, baked shrimp for Greg. Only one couple, probably in their early 30s, seemed to recognize Allie. They smiled and nodded to her on a couple occasions before she smiled, discretely waved, and nodded back. No one approached her during their meal or as they left.

Darkness was fast approaching by the time they returned to the house. They settled in the living room, on a sofa that faced the glass wall, after Greg poured them each a glass of Moscato. He re-opened their earlier conversation by asking Allie what she would miss about her work if she were to retire. She thought for a moment and took a big breath.

"I think the thing I would miss the most would be the songwriting. I enjoy doing that by myself, of course, but I also have so many great writers that I've written with over the years. It's always fun when we get together, and usually we turn out something decent for me to do, for them to record, or to send to someone else."

"Of course, you could still do that," Greg offered. "No matter where you're living, they could come to you. Some place like the beach can be very inspiring. Or you could go to them."

"You're right." Allie smiled and nodded. "I could, and probably would want to do at least a little of that." She paused for a second. "I think I'd also miss the philanthropy part. I enjoy helping deserving people and organizations through the foundation I set up. I used to enjoy showing up for appearances, or to deliver the check. Lately though, the director of the foundation writes the check, and I just sign a letter to go along with it. I guess part of me misses the personal part of that."

"And you could still do that," Greg said. "It's going to take a long time to give away that 98 percent." They both grinned. "Having time to get back to the personal involvement with the foundation would be a wonderful way to slowly and gracefully bow out, but continue to do the good works associated with your name."

"You're right. I would enjoy that." Allie sipped her wine for a moment. "I think I would also enjoy collaborating with other artists once in a while. I always love it when someone asks me to do a duet with them, or just sing backup on a song they're doing." After a moment she added, "I guess I could still do that, too."

"No reason why not. If you get rid of all the other performance related time, the touring, recording, rehearsals, making the videos, and all the appearances to support the new recordings, you'd have a lot of time to have a personal life, a love life, and still do these other things. Just the things you enjoy doing. Right?"

Greg realized he was losing what little objectivity he could have claimed at the beginning of their conversation a few hours ago. He was pretty sure Allie was aware of that too.

"You're right. All that sounds wonderful. It would take some time, of course. I've got this album we've been working on, and I'm pretty well committed to the tour after its release. That's scheduled for this fall in the U.S. and winter in Europe, assuming COVID is under control by then. But, I could let my people know where I'm headed and announce that as my farewell tour. And we could use the time between now and then to work on getting out of all the other things. By this time next year I could be . . ."

"A free woman. Sort of."

"Yeah." Her gaze drifted to the ceiling for a moment. "I think most of the endorsement contracts end either this year or next. It would be a rough year, dealing with everyone's objections and questions. But, I think . . . I think I could do it." When she turned to look at him this time her blue eyes were gleaming. He couldn't quite read what was behind them.

Greg pulled his eyes away from hers, and stared out toward the darkness and the ocean for a second. Then he turned to her and said, "Alison, why don't you just close your eyes for a minute, and try to get in touch with what it would feel like to have your life back? To have time to do what you want to do. And to live where you want to live." He thought about adding, "And to be loved, and in love," but decided not to.

Allie nodded her head, then leaned back and closed her eyes. After just a few seconds, she slid across the sofa, pressed her body into his, and put her head on his shoulder. He wrapped his arms around her and held her tight. They sat in silence for several minutes, each lost in their own thoughts.

Opening Night

"Mr. Aoki, I can't tell you how excited we all are about this exhibition. The gallery staff, from top to bottom, feel honored that you would allow us to be the first to show your wonderful photographs. This is truly groundbreaking. For the world of art, and especially for D.C.." Walt Ackerman was all smiles as they stood in the two-story atrium. They were almost alone, only a few stragglers had yet to file into the auditorium.

His companion nodded slowly. "I'm certainly pleased we could make this happen. But, if you insist I call you Walt, you must call me Nori. It will be interesting to see what names the media has for me tomorrow."

Walt's momentary puzzlement encrusted his face, then disappeared a moment later, replaced by the animated smile again. He edged slowly down the marble-floored hallway. "Well, I'm sure we'll have many chances to talk over the next three months. After the opening tonight we hope you'll stop by frequently, not just for the member's gala and the director's festival, but as often as you're in the area. I'm sure everyone who comes to see your photographs would love to meet you and hear your stories as well."

"I'll see what I can do," Nori said through a cryptic smile, trying his best to keep breathing.

Walt nodded his response, then stopped his shuffle, glanced at his Rolex, and turned to his charge. They were only four minutes after the appointed start time. "I understand we're at capacity, about 300 people, including at least one senator and the special guests you invited. And more media than we really expected." The smile was back again. "I've got to ask, how are you feeling now, before this opening, and your introduction to the world?"

Nori took a moment. Not to think, but to force some saliva down his throat. "I feel a little like . . . I'm back in Afghanistan again."

He was boots on the ground in Kabul, Afghanistan on October 19, 2010. Exactly one year, nine months, and seven days ago. With a Bachelor's degree in visual arts, and three years' experience as a freelance photographer covering the Outer Banks from his home in Kinnakeet, North Carolina, he was ill-prepared for the experience he had talked his way into photographing the U.S. and coalition troops involvement in a war that had been ongoing for decades. He waited until the autumn to go, in part so he'd miss the 100-degree plus temperatures of the Afghan summer. His research told him to expect weather for the next few months in the southern part of the country similar to what he'd experienced during his college days in Arizona.

The materials he'd read about being a photojournalist in a war zone covered a few basics, like protect your camera over anything except your life, since it would not be replaceable. You lose it, or it's damaged beyond your ability to fix it, and you're out of a job and on your way home. The two books he'd read by experienced and respected photojournalists provided little real help, since a war fought in the jungle of Southeast Asia was a world apart from the war in the desert and mountains of Afghanistan.

The biggest help was the photographer, recently home from the war as a result of multiple pieces of shrapnel in the back and buttocks, who gave him 30 minutes on the phone from his bed in a rehabilitation facility. He shared with Nori the importance of establishing relationships with command officers, who would largely determine access to front line positions, as well as fellow photojournalists who could provide up-to-date information on where the Taliban was most active. He said they could also get you educated on the military's official, and unofficial, rules of covering combat. These changed frequently, depending on who you were talking to.

His most practical advice was to act like you belonged there and carry lots of data cards for your camera in your vest. He promised the 300, or even 600, images those cards held in a high-end camera might seem like a lot at home, but would fill up in no time over there.

He added that it was imperative to keep your head down in combat situations and don't try to be a hero or get that once-in-a-lifetime photo. Keeping that passing bullet out of your head, and living another day, was much more important. Then he shared that his wounds came while he was lying face down on the side of a road during a mortar attack. If he had been standing, or even had his head up, watching the action, or trying to take a picture, he had no doubt he would have come home in a box instead of on a stretcher.

A computer-savvy friend helped Nori make an I.D. that looked somewhat like the ones photojournalists from organizations like the New York Times and Washington Post were wearing. This identified him as a representative of the A.P.I.. If anyone asked, he'd declare he was with the American Photojournalists Initiative, a non-existent organization. He figured this was close enough to the Associated Press (A.P.) and the United Press International (U.P.I.), each of which had multiple photographers in the country. The laminated badge hanging from the lanyard had his very Japanese looking face front and center, an American flag in one bottom corner, and a bar code that linked to nothing in the other. He hoped that with this I.D., and his southern accent, he wouldn't be considered much of a security risk.

Eleven minutes later, after an introduction that included the part he had written, but at least three laudatory paragraphs he had not seen, heard, or approved, Nori stepped to the podium and waited a minute for the applause to subside. He noted with relief the glass of water on the shelf below the face of the podium where he laid his notes. He took another several seconds to look over the audience. He had never seen so many tuxedos and evening gowns, but quickly reassured himself that it didn't matter. He took a deep breath, adjusted the microphone slightly, and began.

"Ladies and gentlemen, let me first thank each and every one of you for being here this evening. And thank you for dressing up for the occasion. Even though I didn't." He stepped to the side of the podium, held his arms out, and briefly modeled his white cotton pants and open-necked blue-striped dress shirt. He'd decided, when he'd considered the evening, he would sweat enough without a tight collar and jacket. He wasn't sure which he was dreading more – this talk or the meet-and-greet at the reception as people left the gallery.

"And let me thank the wonderful staff here at the Corcoran Gallery. They've worked tirelessly and graciously over the last month to put this exhibit together. Especially Mr. Walt Ackerman who has walked me though every step of this process." Another pause to allow for polite applause and a sip of water.

"This is the first showing of this collection of photographs, and I hope not the last." He paused for a moment, then half-mumbled, "We'll see." Thankfully, the audience chuckled their acknowledgement of what they perceived as humor.

"It was suggested that I talk a little about the unique nature of the exhibit. I think that's a good way to start, because these photographs are displayed in a number of unusual ways.

"Some are printed on traditional photo paper then matted and framed. Selected ones are printed on very non-traditional paper, such as rice paper, and even handmade paper from Nepal. Some are printed on metal. A few are on canvas and look very much like paintings. The last few are presented quite differently, and I'll explain why in a couple minutes. I chose the manner in which to present the photographs according to how I thought they would make the best impact on the viewer. I hope you'll appreciate the various mediums as you view the photos.

"But, more than this, what I believe really makes these photographs special, is the story they tell. It's a story you may like, or dislike.

They tell a war story, or an anti-war story. The photographs are important and must be seen . . . or they are horrible and should be hidden away. The story they tell is up to you.

"They are here, quite frankly, to provoke controversy. They are here to make you think, to make you feel, and to get you talking about the things you see in these images. It will be quite interesting to read and hear what our friends in the media, who are present with us this evening, will have to say about what they see."

As he studied the faces in front of him, Nori saw there were many encouraging smiles, but also a few expressions of concern. The publicity for this event had been purposely a bit vague. The patrons were promised only an opportunity to be the first to see an important exhibit of photos from the war far away in Afghanistan. A collection that the gallery had fought hard to be the first to display. They were lured in with the promise that they would feel honored to be the first to hear the story of the photos and view them in person. The advertising made it clear no children would be allowed in the gallery.

Nori did not feel particularly flattered by the packed house. He had little doubt that 300 patrons would show up to any opening event the Corcoran advertised.

He took a breath and continued. "I'd like to briefly introduce the collection of images and talk in a little more depth about a few of them. Because of the nature of these photographs, it may be difficult for me to . . . well, I'll just ask you to bear with me." With a step back from the podium, Nori closed his eyes and fought to suppress the wave of emotions that assaulted him frequently over there, and which had infected his brain ever since.

He got to Afghanistan as a result of luck, calling in favors, and promising six large regional newspapers "exclusive" access to his photos for a small up-front fee. He hitched a ride from the airport in Kabul on an Army transport vehicle to the headquarters of the 101st Airborne Division in Helmand Province, in the southern part of the country. It took three days for him to get his first ride-along with a company headed out on patrol.

He quickly learned photographers attached to the military got first priority whenever there was room in a truck. Those from the A.P., U.P.I., or newspapers, (especially the New York Times) were next in line. Photographers from other coalition countries got top priority whenever forces from their country were heading out.

After 11 days and three trips out from the base, he finally saw his first action. The second truck in the convoy he was in hit an IED and seconds later gunfire came from the sand dunes and brush on each side of the road. He and five soldiers in his truck managed to get out and find cover. Nori spend most of the next 10 minutes with his heart on overdrive and his head and body buried in as much sand as he could burrow into. He stuck his arm up once to snap a few pictures, none of which later proved to be usable. He did get photos in the aftermath of the damaged truck, and injured soldiers being cared for and evacuated in choppers.

When he tried to get a photo of the one dead soldier he was rudely pushed away by a captain and told to, "Get the hell out of here!" Back at camp when he told another photographer about this he was informed that the military's rule was you were not allowed to photograph a military casualty in a way that the person could be identified. Faces and name tags were strictly off-limits.

He was afraid he may have committed a major breach that would get him barred from accompanying further operations, but that didn't happen. He made several other trips out on missions, witnessed a lot of brief skirmishes, and a few prolonged battles. He quickly learned the ropes. The soldiers loved to have him take photos of dead enemy troops.

As Nori stepped back to the podium, he stared straight ahead. This time trying not to look into the faces in front of him. He wanted to come across as strong and in control of his emotions, which he most certainly wasn't.

"The photos you'll see in the gallery came from my seven months in Afghanistan as a freelance photojournalist. I left Afghanistan rather abruptly as a result of an injury sustained during the May 7, 2011 attack on the city of Kandahar by the Taliban.

"Most of the photos you will see were taken during, or shortly after, combat operations between the Taliban forces and the coalition forces, made up of United States, Afghanistan, British, Canadian, and Australian troops. A handful of other countries, mostly from NATO, supplied a few troops or logistical support during the time I was there."

He decided it was time for a brief history lesson and a little perspective.

"If you think about it, throughout the history of mankind, war is essentially about one side trying to impose its will on the other through the use of force. There has always been a lot of death and destruction during war – destruction of land, buildings, homes, body parts, and people's lives. War is a brutal thing." He paused for a breath. "And if a photographer is present, and wants to tell the truth, that's what his or her photographs are going to show . . . The ugly truth of war. That's what my photographs show."

Again, Nori stopped to take a breath and gather himself. He looked down at his notes, which were already useless. He'd prepared them in case he lost his nerve and wanted to tread lightly. He returned his gaze to the back wall. His left hand unconsciously rubbed his side, where two pieces of shrapnel had left deep scars.

"I took slightly over 6000 photographs while I was in Afghanistan. You will be seeing either 33, or 37 of these, depending on how much of the reality of this war you want to experience."

After a few weeks, he moved from the 101st headquarters to smaller bases located in, or just outside, small outlying towns around the neighboring providence. There were fewer photographers at these bases, sometimes none. Over the next four months he saw and photographed lots of action, both with units out on missions, and when Taliban forces attacked the various base camps and outposts he traveled to. Each time, the sound of the first gunshot or rocket propelled grenade explosion, or the blast of a vehicle hitting an IED, produced a rush of adrenaline.

The time under fire was both exciting and terrifying. He had two occasions when he was certain his death was moments away. One when he was within 25 yards of a charging Taliban soldier firing a semi-automatic rifle. The second was when he was thrown violently from the back of a jeep as it overturned after hitting an IED. Miraculously, both he and his camera survived with only a few scratches.

But as time went on, he decided that he had put himself in this situation, and if he was going to die, he might as well die doing something he considered important. Like the other photojournalists, and many of the soldiers he talked to, he adopted the attitude that when your time was up your time was up, and there was nothing you could do about it. Part of him felt like that was a self-deceptive lie. But it was a useful one, under the circumstances. Nevertheless, he often found himself silently praying, "Please, let me live through this one."

He also decided he wasn't going to "play it safe," despite the advice he was given by the injured photographer. He wanted to be out on the patrol missions, where the action was. He was going to take the difficult pictures showing the harsh, bloody reality of the troops in combat situations. Many of the other photographers seemed to be content to spend their time on the base, photographing supply activities, soldiers relaxing by tossing a football, or interactions between the troops and the locals, especially children. There was nothing wrong with that. It was part of the story of the war. But not the part he wanted to spend his time on.

As much as he tried to be where the action was, there was a lot of time when absolutely nothing was happening. He used these hours, and sometimes days, to grab a shower, make connections with the other one or two photographers who were sometimes around, sort through his images, and process a few to get ready for his newspaper clients. He cleaned his camera and lenses often to keep the dust from coating the inside of them. This was a never-ending battle.

He decided, after just a couple weeks there, he would always think of Afghanistan as a country with 50 shades of brown. The sand and dirt that was everywhere, the camouflage of the uniforms, trucks, and artillery, the color of the streets and buildings, and the color of skin and clothing after just a few minutes in the ever-present wind outdoors. By the third week he imagined the tissue in his lungs gradually turning brown. He promised himself that after he got home he would never wear brown clothing, live in a brown house, or drive a brown car.

His pictures ran the gamut, from useless (about 90 percent), to interesting but nothing special (about 9 percent), to worth sending back to the papers when he could get internet access (about 1, or maybe 2 percent). He had one series of photographs that truly troubled him.

A cough from the audience made Nori realize how dry his mouth and throat were. Just like they often were over there. He took a quick drink of water, pulled his handkerchief from his pocket for a quick wipe of his forehead, then laid it on top of the pages of notes. He took a deep breath and continued.

"Every photographer strives to take beautiful pictures. Beauty is what people want to look at. All of us. But, when you go into a war zone as a photographer, you know you're not going to be taking beautiful pictures. You can take safe pictures, if you want to. But the real story of warfare is mankind at its worst. And that means photographing death and destruction. And seeing your first dead body is a test . . . A test to see if you have inside you what it takes to be there.

"You've all seen the war movies. When you're there, when you're actually in it, it's not like the movies . . . It's a hundred times worse. But some photos do look like the Hollywood version of war. For the most part, those are the ones that get deleted from your camera, or never go anywhere beyond the hard drive of your computer. Because, after you've been there a while, and taken a few hundred of those, they mean nothing. They lose their impact. Soldiers on stretchers being loaded into a medevac copter with blood stains covering half their uniform. Marines lying face down in the desert sand, their comrades standing around them, staring. Maybe the newspapers or magazines want these. Maybe they're safe enough, sanitized enough for their readers to view.

"A very few photographs give you a real feel of what war is like, and what's it like to be there. Those are the ones that I've selected for you to see in this exhibit. And, let me warn you – this is not for the fainthearted." Nori waited a couple seconds for that message to sink in.

"The soldiers in this particular war were, or I should say, are, since the war is still very much on-going, all volunteers. They signed up knowing there was a risk they would be on the ground in a war zone. This war zone. But, when they get killed or wounded, it's very real – for them, for their comrades-in-arms, for their families and friends back home. The screams of pain, and the agony they go through when they know they're dying, are no less real because they signed up to take the risk.

"Most of the photographs you will see are of these brave soldiers, from the U.S. and coalition forces. You won't be seeing their faces. Except for one – a young man weeping beside the body of his best friend who was found three hours after being captured by the Taliban. His face tells the story . . . But you don't need to see the other faces to see the reality of what has happened to them. The reality of this war."

Another pause. And a quick look at the faces in front of him. They were right there. With him.

"However, the first photograph you'll see this evening, when you walk through the door into that gallery, is not of a soldier. It's an almost life-size photo of an Afghanistan civilian. A friend of mine. A friend of many of the troops who served at the base beside the village of Shorabak. A very brave, kind soul, with a new bride . . ." Nori took a moment to close his eyes and force himself to breathe. "He died . . . About two seconds after the photograph you'll see was taken. It's important that you see his face."

While photos identifying military causalities were off-limits, civilian ones were not.

In most towns or villages there were civilians who served as translators or guides when local Afghan troops were not available. While most civilians, including women and old men, were afraid of being seen with the coalition troops, for fear of being identified as an "infidel," there was usually one or two who had witnessed or experienced the atrocities committed by al-Qaeda or the Taliban, and were willing to provide assistance. One of these was a young man with the first name of Abdul-Rahim. He assisted the troops in the coalition-controlled village of Shorabak, near the Pakistan border.

He was a man in his mid-thirties who had a stump where his right hand used to be. Fourteen years earlier, he had the misfortune to catch a woman who was stumbling in the street after tripping over a loose stone. She was the wife of the local police chief, and Abdul-Rahim was accused of fondling her. Not by the woman or her companion, but by a bystander. Since there were other witnesses who claimed nothing of the sort happened, the police chief decided the proper punishment was to have the "offending hand" removed, rather than have Abdul-Rahim executed.

Nori spent many hours with Abdul-Rahim in the security of the buildings inside the small walled-off base at the edge of town. He asked him questions about Afghanistan, the local village, his friends and family, and his beliefs about the war and what post-war Afghanistan would be like. They laughed together and talked about Abdul-Rahim someday coming to America. There was a mutual respect that quickly developed and they considered themselves friends. He reluctantly posed for a handful of portraits, and one evening took Nori to his home in the village where he posed with his bride of three months for a portrait of the couple. Nori promised to have a print made of the photo as soon as he could and get it to him. He always looked for him whenever he returned to the base from time in the field.

Late one afternoon, Abdul-Rahim agreed to take Nori to visit a 95-year-old village elder whom Abdul-Rahim had told him about and Nori wanted to photograph. A mere 90 yards from the walls of the base, Nori skipped ahead a handful of paces and turned to snap a few shots of his friend walking through the village. Just as he brought the camera to his eye and began snapping, a shot rang out. Abdul-Rahim froze for a second, threw his arms out to his side, then began to slowly crumble. A small circle of red appeared on the left side of his shirt just as his knees hit the ground.

It took Nori a couple seconds to realize what he'd just witnessed through the lens of his camera while his finger was pressing the shutter button. When he did, he dove for the ground just as another shot rang out. He scrambled for the cover of a nearby rusting car frame, then huddled in shock with his arms wrapped around his chest for the next several minutes.

The gunshots brought a squad of heavily-armed soldiers in jeeps and Humvees out of the base and the sniper apparently retreated. A medic quickly began offering aid to Abdul-Rahim, but he was already dead. His body was quickly bagged, then turned over to the Afghan security forces who appeared from the interior of the village. Nori didn't even think to photograph any of this.

By this point, he had photographed hundreds of images of wounded soldiers, and dead ones wrapped in bandages or zipped in body bags, and even a few images of bloody civilian victims of a car bomb.

While the early ones often made him choke, or have to look away as he processed the images on the computer at night, he thought over time he'd developed some degree of immunity to the blood, gore, and mangled body parts he'd seen with his naked eye and captured in the photographs. But, the images in his camera at this moment were ones he didn't want to see, and wasn't sure he'd ever be able to face on the harsh, cold screen of his laptop.

After he got a ride the short distance to the base, and assured the hardened soldiers who came to comfort him that he was okay, he made his way to his cot. He took the data card from the camera and buried it inside a rolled-up pair of clean socks in his duffel bag, then quietly sobbed for the next half-hour. He knew he was responsible for Abdul-Rahim's death. The chaplain attached to the base came to check on him, but he wasn't ready to talk to anybody.

After two days of grieving inside the sheltered walls of the base, and many hours debating whether he should pack it up and go home, he decided he had to get back into doing what he came there to do. But, he knew he could no longer travel into the streets of Shorabak, even in a truck or armored vehicle, as he would have to pass the spot he could no longer face. A day later he hitched a ride on a supply helicopter returning to the city of Kandahar, further inland and under tighter coalition control.

After a few days of hanging around the large base, and slowly getting back into accompanying units out into the surrounding hills on missions, he met a Canadian photographer, Becca Patton. She had been in country four months longer than he had. She was only the second female photojournalist he'd run into.

His first impression of her was that she was tough as nails. She was about 5'4" and maybe all of 125 pounds in full field-ready camouflage khaki pants and shirt, topped by a much-weathered brown photographer's vest. She shot the same Canon camera he did, but, he figured, probably a lot better.

They went out with different units during the day, but ran into each other often in the evenings at the mess tent or the media bivouac area. There was no doubt Nori was still grieving and somewhat withdrawn, but he found Becca easy to talk to. Mostly they compared notes about their day and occasionally shared a picture or two on the small screen on the back of their cameras.

For reasons rooted in his childhood, and the differences in emotional availability of his mother and father, Nori had always found it easier to talk to women than men, and Becca had an amiable, feminine quality to her when she let her guard down. He couldn't imagine the challenges of being a woman in this horrible war zone, surrounded by 95 percent male troops, in a country very callous toward females. But, Becca downplayed the difficulties and said the other women in the area, many of them journalists and nurses, but also a few soldiers attached mostly to supply units, looked out for each other as much as they could.

On the fifth evening they were comparing notes, Becca picked up on his depressed mood and asked how he was weathering the emotional storm of what they were doing and witnessing. He stumbled with his answer for a moment before deciding to be honest and tell her about Abdul-Rahim. She listened for several minutes as he poured out the story, accentuated with a few, quickly wiped, tears.

He admitted to the guilt he still felt and the long nights of the scene playing over and over in his head.

She comforted him with the right words, a hand on his shoulder, and stressed how normal his feelings were. She shared that she'd seen a couple of deaths, and quite a few injuries, of soldiers she'd gotten to know to some degree, but hadn't experienced anything with quite the emotional intensity of what he had. Several months ago, she'd decided not to get closer than a casual greeting to any combatants, simply as a self-protective measure.

Eventually, she asked about the pictures he'd taken of Abdul-Rahim's death. He admitted he hadn't been able to view them. She understood why, but offered to take a look at them, if he'd like. It wasn't until three days later that he brought her the data card.

The next evening, she gave it back to him and told him the five images were hard to look at, knowing what he'd told her, but at the same time remarkable. They evoked a mixture of feelings inside her unlike any pictures she'd ever taken, and only a couple she'd ever seen – Nick Ut's picture of terrified children running away from a napalm attack in Viet Nam, and especially Robert Capa's photograph of a soldier at the moment of a bullet's impact during the Spanish civil war. She asked if he'd thought about what he was going to do with them, and he quickly replied he hadn't.

She said the images needed to be seen. They carried a powerful message about the war, about Afghanistan, about life, and death. A message words couldn't possibly convey.

She told him he was lucky to be freelancing, as was she, because anyone under contract with a newspaper or other organization, or attached to the military, was required to turn over any photos they took. They had no right to use their images personally, and no copyright on them. She added that one of the first things she was going to do when she got home was talk with one of her sponsors, Canada's largest newspaper, about selecting some of her best photographs and putting them together for a show in a gallery in Montreal. She said while she hoped she never shot an image like the ones she'd seen on his card, if she did, at least one of them would be the feature photo of the exhibit.

At 3:00 a.m. the next morning, Nori decided to look at the photos. He'd been unable to sleep that night, and was pretty sure he wouldn't be able to for the indefinite future, now that the emotions had been stirred up again, and his mind kept replaying the conversation with Becca about them.

He cried himself to sleep after viewing each image for just three seconds – all that he could bear.

"The next images you'll see after Abdul-Rahim, are of young men having the worst day of their lives. For some of them, it was the last day of their life. Others would live, but go home missing an arm, or a leg . . . Or both. Or, with a mostly intact body that will feel nothing but pain for the rest of their life."

Nori felt the wetness dripping from under his arms and running from his forehead. He did a quick wipe of his face with the handkerchief, taking a moment to take a sip of water as well.

"They were the unlucky ones. For you see, many of the deaths and injuries that occur during a war like this one are what I came to think of as arbitrary. Mortars, rocket propelled grenades, IEDs, car bombs, and suicide bombers don't target a specific person. They're capricious and indiscriminate. One person dies, and their picture is in the gallery behind you. The one standing three feet away, or riding in the back seat instead of the front, goes on to live another day, fight another battle . . . and go home to hug a wife and children."

Over the next nine days, Nori made six trips into the field. The fighting he witnessed was the most intense he'd seen. He shot nearly 2000 photographs. Many of these were of men running, yelling, diving for cover, firing their weapons, or dragging their wounded comrades to safety. Some were a lot worse. By his count, nine of the coalition soldiers he was with died. Twenty-eight were seriously wounded. He didn't want to count the number of Taliban troops killed. The pictures he took were some of the most graphic.

During the last day, he was caught in the middle of a deadly two-hour firefight between coalition and Taliban troops, complete with artillery bombardment and intense air support by a small fleet of helicopters. After viewing his images of the battle, Nori decided he'd taken enough pictures of death, disfigurement, and the horrors of war for a while. Since he had no deadlines for submitting pictures, or real obligations to anyone beside himself, he decided to take a break. Maybe for a week, or two. He'd miss the excitement, but he promised himself he'd be back.

He informed Becca the next evening that he was going to spend a few days in the city of Kandahar looking for, and photographing, beauty in the war-torn city. She jumped on the idea and immediately told him he should do it. She told him she might consider doing the same at some point, and added she was looking forward to seeing his photos whenever they met. She promised not to show him any more of her photos from the field.

For the next week, Nori spent each day wandering the streets of ancient Kandahar from sunrise to sunset. He was surrounded by many more shades of brown, but there was nevertheless a great deal of beauty throughout the city.

He was cautious at first, and felt awkward and out of place. But over time became more comfortable taking pictures and communicating, mostly with gestures, with the people who were not afraid of him. His eyes gradually began to see beauty in the faces of the children he met, and the faces full of both wisdom and pain in the elders, who had lived most of their lives surrounded by war.

He captured images of birthday parties in the residential area streets and religious celebrations he had no reference for understanding. He sat on benches in parks and watched children playing soccer, snapping pictures of their smiling and laughing faces as they ran by. There was color in the buildings, paint on the doors, and some brightness in the clothing – reds, greens, blues, instead of the usual browns and blacks so prominent in the smaller towns and villages.

Twice, he came across gardens with newly blooming marigolds, poppies, and nasturtiums in raised gardens of soil, likely brought in from the mountain region to the north. Trees were few, except for a few young ones bunched together in carefully tended plots. However, the city had famers' markets with an abundance of grapes, melons, and pomegranates grown on irrigated farmland to the west of the city near the Arghandab River.

While many of the buildings, especially in the Old City district, had been destroyed by decades, and even centuries of war, a few had managed to remain free of damage and were quite magnificent by any standard. Nori spent a full hour photographing the Mosque of the Cloak of the Prophet Mohammed with its striking blue dome and blue and green tile walls. The next day it was two hours photographing the mausoleum of Ahmed Shah Durrani, with its marvelous green gilded dome, and the 12 lesser tombs of his children that surrounded it.

He felt his spirits lifting with each passing day. The emotions of evenings spent reviewing his photos, with Becca looking over his shoulder whenever she was available, were in sharp contrast to the earlier times viewing images of warfare and destruction. These photos had color, life, history, and joy. His depression was virtually gone. He was sleeping well, and looking forward to each new day and the discoveries it promised.

"The last set of photographs in this exhibit are set off from the others behind a partition. Just before you enter that area, if you chose to do so, you will see a portrait of another photographer, Becca Patton. I'm sure you'll see the toughness behind her smiling face. It is she, and not I, who took that last group of photos.

"They are quite dramatic, and many, perhaps all, of you will find them difficult to view. I've chosen to present them as a brief slide show displayed on a large computer monitor mounted on the wall. Each of the four images will remain visible for three seconds, with two seconds in-between. I ask that you enter the viewing area during the one minute the monitor is blank, and exit during the one minute of blank screen after. About 15 of you at a time can stand in the viewing area."

It took Nori several seconds to swallow the lump in his throat.

"Those images are the last ones Becca took before she died. They were taken in the last seconds of her life, and just a few minutes after the portrait of her was taken. She died in the middle of a street in Kandahar, Afghanistan on May 7th, 2011. Just before she died, she asked me to take the images and do something meaningful with them . . . I've chosen to share them with you."

On the eighth day of what Nori had come to think of as his healing odyssey, Becca found him in the pre-dawn morning and announced that she would like to join him. She felt the need for a break from the tension of her daily trips into the hillsides and dusty plains with the coalition troops, and the increasing level of engagement with Taliban troops that seemed to be happening. She had witnessed what walking the city streets and photographing beauty had done for Nori.

He accepted her offer of companionship with delight. There were numerous sights he wanted her to see and a couple interesting spots he had yet to visit. After a quick breakfast and packing a light lunch, they filled their vests with lenses and their canteens with water, and journeyed out. They stopped for a few minutes beside one of the flowerbeds and took portraits of each other.

They had walked perhaps a mile, and taken a handful of photos, when they heard the first explosions. They both recognized the sounds of mortars and rocket-propelled grenades. The first blasts were coming from their left, near a police station about a mile away. The next round, much closer, came from the area of the high school, to their right.

As they turned to look at each other, Nori was the first, by a half-second, to exclaim, "Oh, shit!" They took cover between two buildings near a city market while watching and listening as they tried to figure out what was happening. Instinctively, they both had their cameras at the ready.

Over the next couple of minutes, the bombardment got more intense and closer from each direction. They began to hear small arms fire in nearly every direction, except behind them, the direction of the coalition base. It became clear that the Taliban was mounting an attack on the city.

Over the all-too-familiar sounds of warfare, they agreed the best course of action was to retreat toward the base. They stepped out from their cover as rapidly approaching grenade and mortar fire chased small groups of frightened people from the downtown buildings toward them.

Among them was a young woman running down the middle of the street carrying an infant in her arms. As they watched her get closer,

Becca shouted in his ear, "I've got to get this," and jumped out into the street.

Nori shouted, "No!" and tried to grab her, but he caught only the edge of her vest as she tore away from him. He quickly decided he had to follow her and ran out to the street with one hand on his camera. From a few yards behind her, he watched as she dropped to her knees and raised the camera to her eye. He immediately brought his camera to his eye, thinking he would capture an image of her in the foreground, photographing the mother and child as they ran toward her.

At that moment, as Nori pressed the shutter button and watched through the camera lens, a flash of yellow, orange, and red light exploded just a couple yards behind the terrified woman. He watched her fly through the air, the infant thrown violently from her arms. A second later he saw Becca collapse backward and on her right side, her shattered camera landing just behind her head.

After his evacuation, and time in the hospital stateside, Nori returned to his home in Kinnakeet. Once he was able, he walked the beach every day, benefiting over time from the ocean therapy. With the help of a group of kind and loving Kinnakeeters, he healed, mostly, both physically and emotionally.

"It took me a long time after I got home to decide whether to show my images, and the ones from Becca, to anyone . . . Ultimately, I

231

decided people needed to see them. They're an important part of what's happening over there.

"It's clear to me, that people can learn a lot more, and have a chance to really understand the beneath-the-surface reality of something like a war, when pictures accompany, or maybe even take the place of, words. I don't believe any words about this war can have the same impact, carry the same message to your brain, or your heart, as the images you will see this evening. These photographs are of the things nobody back here would see, or have a chance to understand, without a photographer there to capture the scenes as they happen."

Nori closed his eyes for a moment. He felt a quick chill run through him. When he got his eyes open again it took a second for him to refocus.

"I hope you feel something when you see these images. I believe the people in the photographs would want you to feel something. Feel something for them. For the sacrifices they've made. For their lives irreparably changed, or cut short. For their families.

"I want these photos to touch your heart . . . as they have mine. And I hope you'll leave here a changed person, with much to think about, after seeing these images."

Nori leaned with both hands on the podium, then looked slowly, from left to right, at the faces in the audience in front of him. His eyes stopped on a middle-aged woman in the front right corner VIP section. She was quietly sobbing into a fist full of tissues. The man next to her had his arm around her shoulders and his face buried in her neck. A tiny band of light reflecting off the stage caught the small maple leaf pattern on his bow tie. Nori's throat cinched.

"I am honored by your being here," he managed to say, looking directly at them. Then, looking back to the middle of the auditorium, he said, "Thank you for your time."

As he stepped back from the podium, Nori grabbed his handkerchief with a shaky hand and wiped his forehead, then his eyes. The audience remained eerily silent for a full ten seconds before the applause began.

Afterword

I have enjoyed listening to and telling stories my whole adult life.

In my many years as a therapist I listened to people tell the stories of their lives. I also shared stories with them, both real and made-up. These were designed to provide them with hope and guidance, and stimulate their own ideas for problem solving. This well-established technique is known as "therapeutic storytelling."

At home, my children fell asleep many nights listening to my original bedtime stories. Their favorite was about little Ben and Mary, who found a magical house in the forest filled with the most wonderful toys. After playing for hours, they were so tired that they cozied up on the most comfortable beds anyone could ever imagine. Thinking about what a perfect day they'd had, they drifted off to sleep, to have peaceful dreams about how lucky they were. That was one of my favorites too.

For years now I've walked the beaches and neighborhoods of Kinnakeet playing the game in my head of "what if." I made up stories about real and imaginary people. Some were inspired by fishermen I met on the beaches. Some by people who'd escaped their previous lives to live by the ocean and do nothing but listen to the waves and watch the seagulls. Others slipped into my head while just enjoying the beauty around me.

I'm privileged to share some of these stories with you. I hope you enjoy them. Get in touch if you'd like to hear more.

Bernie Lewis
Kinnakeetstories@gmail.com
Find more at Kinnakeet Stories on Facebook

Acknowledgments

I would like to thank my family – wife Debbie, son Cory, and daughter Rian for their continuous love, support, and encouragement of his writing and photography. This book would not be possible without them.

I must also thank the many people who have read my short stories and viewed my photographs over the years. Thank you for both your feedback and encouragement. Especially Angie, Stacy, and Carlan.

Great thanks are also due to Joe Sledge, who's many books on the Outer Banks have educated and entertained me and many others. They are well worth your reading. His publication of this collection of stories and photographs through Gravity Well Books is greatly appreciated.

A special note of appreciation is due to GeeGee Rosell, owner of Buxton Village Books, and the biggest supporter of authors crafting stories of the Outer Banks. Her encouragement and guidance were crucial. Visitors to the Outer Banks are encouraged to visit her bookstore and purchase their reading materials there, or from Buxton Village Books online. Support of this, and your own local independent bookstore, is a critical part of keeping reading and writing alive in our culture.

240

About The Author

Bernie Lewis was born and raised in San Diego, California where he first learned to love and appreciate the beauty of the ocean and coastal environment. He moved east as a young man and has lived the last 40-plus years in Winchester, Virginia. He has been a frequent visitor to the Outer Banks of North Carolina since the age of 20. He and his family have owned a vacation home in Kinnakeet since 2020.

Bernie graduated from Washington and Lee University, then obtained a master's and Ph.D. degrees from the University of Virginia. He ran a private practice as a clinical psychologist for 35 years. He is the author of *Local Heroes: Winchester, Virginia 2000 – 2010* as well as the photo book, *The Long Branch You've Never Seen*. He has been writing short stories for over 15 years. His fascination with photographing the world around him began during his days in high school.

One of his favorite activities is wandering the beaches of Kinnakeet looking for appealing images to capture with his camera and dreaming up interesting stories to tell.

9 789898 801712 7